CURSED COGS

by Angela Roquet

World Clock Journals
Cursed Cogs
Gear Hearts
Time Peace

Lana Harvey, Reapers Inc.
Graveyard Shift
Pocket Full of Posies
For the Birds
Psychopomp
Death Wish
Ghost Market
Hellfire and Brimstone
Limbo City Lights (short story collection)
The Illustrated Guide to Limbo City

Coming December 2021: A Lana Harvey spin-off series Return to Limbo City

Blood Vice
Blood Vice
Blood and Thunder
Blood in the Water
Blood Dolls
Thicker Than Blood
Blood, Sweat, and Tears
Flesh and Blood
Out for Blood
Blood Shots (short story collection)

Spero Heights
Blood Moon
Death at First Sight
The Midnight District

CURSED COGS

WORLD CLOCK JOURNALS BOOK ONE

ANGELA ROQUET

VIOLENT SIREN PRESS

CURSED COGS

Copyright © 2021 by Angela Roquet

All rights reserved.

Cover Design by Rebecca Frank of Bewitching Book Covers

Edited by Chelle Olson of Literally Addicted to Detail

www.angelaroquet.com

ISBN: 978-1-951603-31-1

For Paul and Xavier,

who make my world go round.

*"The work of today is the history of tomorrow,
and we are its makers."*

— Juliette Gordon Low

Prologue

September 13ᵗʰ, 1911 – 11:50 a.m.

Visiting the Huxley workshop never failed to put a spring in Dorian's step and a whistle between his lips. The thick aroma of coffee and grease greeted him as he stepped off the busy sidewalk, and a string of bells hanging from the door announced his arrival.

The vestibule was empty, save for a desk pushed up against the far wall where a stack of mail and a basket of sweating milk bottles waited to be noticed. Much like Dorian waited now, craning his neck to steal a glance through the wide entrance that led to the tinkering floor.

Open books and brass, mechanical creations decorated every tabletop, and while they were generally enough to spark Dorian's delight, something new snagged his notice today. A metal hoop encrusted with purple crystals had been erected in the center of the room, balanced atop a series of wire-wrapped poles. The strange contraption was at least a dozen feet wide, and every so often, a crackle of blue electricity flickered across the void, like a soap bubble attempting to take form, before arcing up toward the atrium's glass ceiling.

"Ah, young Mr. Verne!" Ezra Huxley appeared at the

top of a rickety staircase that led to a lofted living space behind the workshop. A sudden burst of electricity lit his eyes and reflected off the goggles nestled in his hair. For a moment, Dorian saw the mad scientist his pa's customers carried on about in gossipy whispers—though the tattered waistcoat was admittedly less formidable than a white lab jacket.

Mr. Huxley descended the stairs, working a rag over his oil-stained hands. His face stretched with a brilliant smile, a herald of the customary joke that opened their every conversation.

"What time does a duck wake up?"

"I've no idea," Dorian said, yielding without a guess.

"At the *quack* of dawn." Mr. Huxley guffawed at his cleverness and then asked, "What have ya got for me today, my good sir?"

"Just some old junk my pa said was taking up too much space." Dorian's face flushed as he handed over the crate of busted gears and clock parts. "He said to ask for two dollars but that I could go as low as one."

Mr. Huxley chuckled. "Not much for haggling, are ya?" When Dorian looked down at his feet, the man gave his shoulder a playful slap. "Me either, kid. I like a straight shooter." He took a quick poke through the rubbish and clicked his tongue. "I tell ya what… Why don't we split the difference?"

"Really?" Dorian's cheeks felt hot again. "But it's just a bunch of garbage. I don't want to take advantage—"

"Nonsense!" Mr. Huxley held up a bent pendulum from a grandfather clock that hadn't survived being dropped off a delivery ship at the wharves. "I can think of at least three uses for this piece alone."

"You're lying," Dorian insisted, though a grin had crept over his face.

The bells on the door jingled again, and Isla Huxley's musical laughter sent a thrill through Dorian that he nearly blamed on the new invention. He shot the device a cautious glare, but his interest soon shifted to the red-headed girl.

Freckles dotted her nose and cheeks, tinged pink despite the wide-brimmed hat she wore. The adornment sat slanted on her head, feathers and silk flowers piled at the crown like a bow atop a gift. Her frilly, cream-colored dress reminded Dorian of the cakes his ma used to make every year for his birthday.

Mrs. Huxley wore a similar hat and dress, though in a dusty violet color that complemented the purple pendant hanging from a cord around her neck. Dorian wondered if it had been cut from a crystal like those wired together over the tinkering floor. It was lovely, and it reminded him that Isla would turn fifteen next month. He'd have to find a suitable gift. Hopefully, something that could express his evolving affection better than the words he so often garbled in her presence.

Dorian had always found Isla to be the most interesting creation in the Huxley workshop, but he couldn't remember ever having such a hard time hiding it. Thankfully, she didn't seem to notice. Or she didn't care. He wasn't sure which, and he was too afraid to ask.

"Captain Gear Heart!" The paper grocery sack in Isla's arms crinkled as she squeezed it tighter. "Do you come bearing treasure?"

Dorian's ears burned at the nickname she'd given him when they were children, playing pirates and sea monsters in the workshop. Back when his only responsibilities had been winding the street clocks and delivering spare parts to Mr. Huxley. Before his ma had succumbed to tuberculosis and his pa had needed more help in the store.

"It's just some old junk," Dorian confessed again, stuffing his hands into his trouser pockets. He didn't know what else to do with them now that he wasn't holding the crate, and his palms had begun to sweat.

"We'll give it a nice new home," Isla said as if he'd brought them a kitten instead. "Oh! You should stay for lunch. Do you like blushing bunny with tomato soup?" She took a step closer and lowered her voice before adding, "We made chocolate brownies this morning to celebrate Father's new machine. Have you seen it? Isn't it wonderful?"

"Isla, give the boy a chance to answer one question before you go asking him ten more." Mrs. Huxley offered Dorian an apologetic smile as she nudged her daughter aside. She waited for Mr. Huxley to set the crate of parts on the desk and then handed off a second paper sack of groceries to him before turning to close the shop door, muffling the car horns and clopping hooves on the street outside.

"Well?" Isla asked expectantly. "Will you stay?"

"I... I don't..." Dorian looked to Mr. Huxley for help, suddenly unable to make words.

"I'll tell your pa you drove a tough bargain next time I see him. Surely he understands a good deal takes time and care," he said with a wink.

"Right." Dorian nodded. "Besides, he's got Pearl there to help if it gets busy."

"She's such a sweet girl." Mrs. Huxley sighed and pinched the fingertips of her crocheted gloves, delicately removing them. "And so smart. I can't believe how quickly she picked up the trade."

"Has she started talking yet?" Isla asked.

"No." Dorian pressed his lips together and tried to smile. It was hard when thinking about Pearl. He hadn't agreed with his pa's decision to adopt her, but that wasn't Pearl's fault. And for what it was worth, she *had* lightened his workload. "Dr. Doyle says she might never speak," he added. "But he's teaching her how to talk with her hands—not that it'll be much use with customers."

Isla's nose crinkled. "They didn't teach her how to do that at the asylum before she came to live with you and Mr. Verne?"

"No, but she did learn to read and write, and they let her keep a slate for asking and answering questions," Dorian said. "Pa hated it. The noise gave him headaches. He threw it out and got her a journal and penny pencil to use instead."

"The poor dear." Mrs. Huxley stroked the pendant hanging from her neck. "I wish there was more we could—"

The bells on the door rang out, cutting her off as a bearded man in a black suit and Homburg hat entered the workshop. Gold glinted from the stickpin in his ascot, the eagle head of his cane, and the chain dangling from his pocket, where Dorian suspected he carried a watch much finer than any on display at his pa's store.

"Orwell," Mr. Huxley said by way of greeting, his jaw flexing stiffly. "What a pleasant surprise."

"Good Lord." The man's eyes narrowed on the ring of crystal above the tinkering floor. "I didn't want to believe it—the things they're saying on the street—but there's no denying it now, Ezra. You've gone completely mad!"

"Mind your manners, Abraham." Mrs. Huxley gripped Isla's shoulder and dragged her back a step, moving to put herself between her daughter and the newcomer. "That's no way to speak to family."

"Family?" He snorted. "You stopped being family the day you traded your good name for this crackpot's."

Mr. Huxley turned on his heel and headed toward the stairs at the back of the shop, a grocery sack still nestled in his arms. "The science is sound," he called over his shoulder. "I suppose you'll want to have a look before deciding how much to invest."

"Invest?" Orwell scoffed. "What on earth makes you think I'd ever consider—"

"Why else would you be here?" Mr. Huxley paused at the base of the steps, but he didn't look back. "If this isn't a social call, that leaves only one explanation. Or two, I suppose, if *you've* gone mad."

Orwell made a noise in the back of his throat that

suggested he had considered the possibility himself. He passed his cane from hand to hand and eyed the door. When he spotted Isla, his gaze softened, though only briefly. A deep crease cut across his brow as his attention migrated to Dorian. "There is some other business we might discuss while I'm here."

Mr. Huxley was already out of earshot and halfway up the stairs, but Mrs. Huxley picked up where he'd left off.

"The drawings are all laid out on the dining table. Why don't you come up and have a look while I prepare luncheon?" She aimed a gentle smile at Dorian before stashing her gloves in her pockets and taking the second bag of groceries from Isla. "I'll call you two up when it's ready."

Dorian nodded, unable to find his voice under the scrutiny of the great Abraham Orwell. He'd never seen the man in person, but everyone knew the name of the domineering tycoon who had taken Boston's Best by storm.

"I really haven't the time for nonsense," Orwell grumbled. "I'd much rather hear your plans for Isla's future schooling."

"Her weekly lessons with Winifred are far superior to anything she might learn at the schoolhouse," Mrs.

Huxley countered.

"No, no." Orwell waved his cane dismissively. "I don't mean *public* school. Good heavens."

"Oh. I see. Well…" She readjusted the bag of groceries on her hip and gathered up the milk bottles before heading for the stairs. "We'll have to discuss it in the loft. This meal isn't going to cook itself. And since you're here," she added, her voice perking, "you might as well have a look at the designs for the new machine."

"I'm not agreeing to anything," Orwell insisted. "Even if such a device were to work—which I very much doubt—there are a great many other factors to consider."

"Take your time," Mrs. Huxley shouted back. "But you should know, one of Edison's men was sniffing around early this morning. And Ezra has patron appointments scheduled all next week. This may be your only chance to have a proper look before it's old news."

"Very well." Orwell huffed and stalked after Mrs. Huxley, taking his time on the rickety stairs and muttering under his breath the whole way. Dorian waited for them to disappear through the arched loft entrance before closing his gaping mouth and turning back to Isla.

"You're related to Abraham Orwell?" he rasped under his breath.

Isla nodded grimly. "My uncle. Though we hardly ever see him." She removed the pins from her hat and slipped it off, knocking a curl loose from the nest of hair she'd been wearing up more lately than down. Dorian's gaze fell to her neck, tracing a line from her ear lobe to the hollow at the base of her throat.

"What is it?" Isla fingered the lace on her collar. "Did I spill coffee on my frock?"

"No… I mean… I don't think so." His ears felt as if they were being seared to his head, and each breath took more effort to draw than the last.

Isla glanced up slowly, her honey-colored eyes peeking through dark lashes. "Are you well, Dorian? You seem out of sorts."

He opened his mouth to answer, but a ruckus from the loft snapped his focus away.

"She belongs at a finishing school," Orwell bellowed. "How do you expect her to find a proper husband after the way you've brought her up here—just shy of a feral cat."

"A finishing school?" Dorian echoed. His head swam at the idea. "Like the ones for court ladies over in Europe?"

Isla laughed. "Don't worry. They've had this argument before. Mother and Father are entirely opposed.

I'm not going anywhere. Besides, Winnie's lessons are far more useful than any of the silly things they teach at those charm schools."

The shouting picked up again in the loft, but the subject had changed to the new invention. Namely, how ridiculous it was. How it couldn't possibly work, and no one would fund it.

Dorian's gaze narrowed on the strange device as another swell of electricity crawled toward the glass ceiling. "It sure is…*unusual.* Do you know what it does?"

"I do." The corners of Isla's eyes crinkled. She sucked in her bottom lip and clutched her hat over her chest. "It's a time machine," she whispered.

Dorian rolled his eyes. "We're a little old for make-believe."

"I'm serious," she squealed, though a giggle bubbled through her words. "Look there." She pointed at the ring of crystals. "Do you know what those are?"

"Amethysts?" he guessed. His pa stocked the display case with more ornate timepieces around the holidays, pretty locket watches adorned with gemstone beads he'd had to learn the names of in case a customer asked.

"Everyone else thought so too, at first," Isla said. "The subway diggers found a cavern full of them when they were excavating for Atlantic Station and the eastern tunnel—the section where it goes under the harbor." She tossed her hat onto a nearby table and rummaged through a pile of tools and wires, coming away with a stray bit of purple crystal. "One of the local jewelers bought a heap of it from the city before realizing their mistake. It's apparently difficult to work with, full of impurities and whatnot. Father purchased it for a fraction of the original price."

"If not amethyst, what is it?" Dorian asked.

Isla shrugged. "I suppose it doesn't have a name yet. But it vibrates at a different frequency than amethyst, and has elastic pluck—no, that's not right. An elastic…*pleochroism*, I think is what Father called it."

"Right, of course." Dorian dipped his chin in an agreeable nod, deciding to hold out a bit longer rather than confess that he had no inkling what she was carrying on about. Isla's sly grin suggested that she already knew.

"Look closely," she said, holding the chunk of crystal up to catch the sunlight streaming through the atrium glass. "What do you see?"

Dorian snorted, sensing another tribute to their colorful childhood. But then something flickered across a smooth span of the gemstone's surface—a fragment of a face. A wide eye and a mouth forming a startled o.

"Something that's happened already?" Isla pressed. "Or something that's yet to transpire?"

Dorian reached for the crystal, but she pulled away. He caught her wrist instead and tugged it toward his face, searching the odd rock for another peek at whatever it had almost shown him. Isla's breath tickled his neck as her body folded behind his. She rested her cheek against his shoulder, her bright eyes probing the purple quartz for answers, too.

"Father's been obsessed with the Curie brothers' research on crystallography and piezoelectricity," she said, her voice dropping as the shouting upstairs continued. "And some German physicist's writings on spacetime and electrodynamics. He thinks he can manipulate the crystals so that they not only *show* distant fragments of time, but transport one *to* those times. Wouldn't that be something?"

Dorian watched her from the corner of one eye. He admired the way she blossomed like a flower anytime she spoke about her father and his work. He wondered if he'd ever do anything so spectacular that she'd swell with such awe when speaking about him.

A crash sounded from upstairs, likely a chair being overturned, and then Mrs. Huxley appeared on the landing. She blew a loose curl away from her face and grasped her hips with both hands.

"I'm telling you, it's possible," she said. "We can prove it."

"I didn't come here for a performance," Orwell snapped as he stopped in the mouth of the loft entrance. He sliced his cane through the air, pointing the end down at the tinkering floor. "You can save the theatrics for the crystal-ball-gazing carnival-goers. That's the only paying audience you'll find in this city."

"It's nearly ready for a test run," Mr. Huxley said, trying and failing to slip past Orwell. "We'll need a volunteer subject, naturally. I'm sure I'll be able to round up a reliable chap within a day or two."

"We don't need a volunteer for *this* demonstration." Mrs. Huxley made for the stairs, but Orwell snatched her by the sleeve.

"For once, I agree with your husband. Don't be a fool, Elizabeth!"

"You already think me one, so what does it matter?" She bared her teeth at him and wrenched her arm free. The landing trembled at the motion, the metal creaking and groaning as if it were a fourth party in the debate—and prepared to have the last word.

Mrs. Huxley stumbled back a step. The railing connected with her waist, and then she was airborne. Dress flapping about her heels. Eyes wide and mouth forming a startled o.

Just the way Dorian remembered.

But the murky slice of quartz hadn't revealed what came next.

An arc of blue electricity crackled between the crystals. It danced across the void, funneling upward into a precarious cyclone. Then, just as Mrs. Huxley reached the metal ring, she vanished.

Chapter One

December 13ᵗʰ, 1916 – 7:52 a.m.

Hating Dorian was always hardest just before eight o'clock. Not that Pearl thought she could ever *truly* hate him. But the fresh reminder of what they'd almost had made the idea of leaving seem impossible. That nostalgic heartache would diminish soon enough, though.

Just a few more minutes, she thought to herself, her gaze darting between the grandfather clock in the corner and the closed door that led to the storeroom and stairwell to the apartments above. She looked back at the front window in time to witness three eggs splat against the glass, right over the shop name etched in swirling calligraphy. *The Clockwork Apothecary.*

"Gearhead!" someone shouted. Muffled laughter filtered in from the street out front, fading as the young culprits made their escape.

Children were cruel.

It was a universal excuse many an adult had thrust upon Pearl ever since she was old enough to understand that she was different. Even before *the Break.*

If it were true that a gentleman preferred a soft-spoken bride, Pearl supposed she'd have enough suitors to fill the Boston Harbor—that was if ships were still allowed in the harbor. Nary a vessel had touched the slice of horizon visible from the city in at least three months.

It was anyone's guess what excuse the rest of the world had been fed for Boston's sudden withdrawal from civilization. There were plenty of rumors, of course. Secret military preparations for the country's inevitable entry into the war. A polio epidemic that rivaled New York City's. A hostile take-over by the Central Powers. A leprosy outbreak brought on by runaways from Penikese Island.

The truth was far stranger, yet just as dangerous as anything the governor might have told those unafflicted by the Break. The hourly time warps that radiated from the Custom House Tower brought a new kind of sickness to this isolated section of the city—to Late Boston, where a broken time machine rained hell upon poor souls lost to their history.

But not everyone trapped in Late Boston had diverged from the original timeline. Not everyone suffered the same fate or required intervention to survive after the Break. And those fortunate, unscathed few had cast their blame and cruelty upon the mechanical abominations within the city.

Gearhead. Clock slave. Tinker's curse.

In any case, Pearl was no stranger to prejudice. Even something as harmless as a girl with no voice had caused her poor mother enough distress to abandon her at the nearest orphanage. Though the insult had felt like a blessing in disguise after Hugo Verne had taken her in, despite the headmistress's warning that Pearl would be of little use in his store, given her silent disposition.

That's when Pearl had first met Dorian. He'd been fourteen at the time, three years older than her, and full of a familiar melancholy that most adults dismissed by proclaiming a child was wise beyond their years. But for Dorian, it was true. Pearl could tell almost immediately. Her survival hinged on her powers of observation and intuition, and she was rarely wrong about these things. These gifts also made her a fast learner.

Once she'd mastered the household chores, Mr. Verne had tasked her with additional duties in the store. Sweeping the floors and polishing the timepieces was easy work and gave her the opportunity to watch Dorian's careful hands toil over his father's worktable.

Where clockwork was concerned, Dorian was an artist. Mr. Verne had trained him well. His abilities enchanted Pearl, and she'd soon committed every clock part and its function to memory, as well as every tool and its place in the shop. It wasn't long before she began helping with the repair work, leaving Dorian to focus on sales and deliveries—when Mr. Verne felt well enough to manage the store in his son's absence, anyway.

After they had closed for the day and retired upstairs, Pearl would cook dinner, stealing the occasional glance across the room at Dorian where he perched on the wide windowsill, an open book in his lap. He never looked up, not even when they gathered at the dining table to eat.

Pearl supposed she could have snapped her fingers or clapped her hands to summon his attention. But that was how one garnered irritation—not interest. So, she'd been patient, hoping that one day his gaze would lift, and he'd catch her studying him like a tarnished mirror in search of her own reflection. That maybe he would look at her the same way.

She knew Dorian hadn't wanted her. At least, not at first. That much was clear. But Mr. Verne had needed extra help after his wife's death, and the asylum had needed to find Pearl a home. It'd been an ideal arrangement for everyone—except for Dorian.

Pearl had desperately wanted to win him over. Only a few of the customers had taken a shine to her, but she'd found their pity suffocating. And none of them were her age. Dorian didn't have many friends either. Except for Ezra Huxley, the deranged inventor who had designed the machine responsible for Boston's downfall.

Dorian had witnessed the first failed trial. He'd shared the details with his father after returning late one afternoon from making a delivery to the Huxley workshop. How Elizabeth Huxley had vanished into thin air, and how Ezra had completely unraveled. How their daughter had shown him the future in a facet of a crystal without a name.

Mr. Verne had called Dorian a liar and ordered him not to speak of the incident to another soul. Reputation was everything for a business in a big city where a competitor resided on every street corner. Losing credibility could very well mean losing the roof over their heads.

Soon, nasty rumors concerning Elizabeth's disappearance had worked their way through Boston, spreading like poison from one social circle to the next. The whispers were heard in the darkest tavern corners and the brightest tearooms. And, of course, they'd found their way to the modestly lit store counter at the Clockwork Apothecary.

That's when the deliveries to the Huxley workshop had stopped, and Mr. Verne warned Dorian to stay away from the inventor. For a while, Dorian even listened. But Pearl suspected that had more to do with the fact that the Huxley girl had been shipped off to some fancy school in Europe. Ezra was in no condition to care for her, and his workshop was evidently unsafe.

True as that may have been, it didn't help ease Pearl's shame over how delighted she'd been to have Dorian all to herself. Neither did his melancholic mood that stretched on for months after.

But then Fenway Park had opened, and Dr. Doyle, the retired physician who lived in the apartment above theirs, took them to a Red Sox game. They'd sat shoulder to shoulder, trapped in a sea of bodies crushing in on all sides. Pearl had felt paralyzed by the noise and the heat. The sun burned her eyes, and her lungs ached with every breath. Another second, and she would have fainted—if Dorian's hand hadn't found hers, gently squeezing to get her attention.

Would you like some popcorn? he'd signed.

Pearl had been too shocked to answer until she noticed Dr. Doyle's pleased grin.

Rome wasn't built in a day, his hands had replied over Dorian's shoulder. It was an expression the doctor used often—usually when she struggled to learn something new or felt sorry for herself for not having friends her age.

Not that Dr. Doyle wasn't good company. He made the most wonderful sweets and let her have free rein of his personal library, loaning her his most prized medical texts. After which, their conversations grew vastly more interesting.

But Pearl dreamed like any other girl. She wanted to find her place in the world, and she wanted to be loved—not just in a doting, grandfatherly way. She craved the kind of love that made hearts grow wings and take flight. The kind that came with roses and poetry. She wanted someone to find her more lovely than a summer's day.

These didn't seem like such impossible desires. Not for a normal girl, anyway. And Pearl was very much a normal girl, aside from communicating a little differently than most, and having a respectable knowledge of clockwork and medicine.

Unfortunately, Dorian's affection peaked at learning to sign and buying her popcorn at the occasional ball-game. And though he was kinder and more attentive, he still didn't see her the way she saw him. Neither did anyone else.

The years dragged on. Then, Mr. Verne's heart gave out one night, and he passed in his sleep. At the funeral, Dorian had wrapped his arm around Pearl's shoulders and told her that everything would be all right. That she would always have a home and a job at the Clockwork Apothecary.

A few months later, the wedding invitation arrived. Ezra Huxley's daughter was back from Europe and engaged to a French airship captain.

Something shifted in Dorian that day. Something Pearl's intuition told her was about to change their lives forever. Although, she'd confused the dread knotting her guts for butterflies. It wasn't until the big day that she understood just how horribly wrong things would go. For everyone.

And it was Dorian's fault. Of that much, she was sure. His guilt was evidence enough.

Yet, she couldn't bring herself to hate him. Even now, knowing with absolute certainty that he had never loved her—*couldn't* love her—not the way she loved him. No matter how her heart swelled at the memory of his hand on her waist as they danced. His warm lips against her cheek. The necklace he'd given her before the wedding reception, cool and heavy against her flushed skin.

That slice of time was a lie, despite the ghosts that lingered in her mind, rushing out to greet her every time the clock brought them back to life. She prayed for the spell to break, to cut her free from whatever kept her bound to Dorian, longing for a life that he'd almost given her and then snatched away.

Yes, children were cruel.

The golden egg yolk streaked across the front window reminded her again. And while false memories of Dorian broke her heart in this timeline, something else wounded her in the next. Something a bit more fatal than crushed hopes and dreams.

Pearl pried open the face of the brass collar housing the mechanism Dorian had built to revive her after the broken timelines converged. Delicate cogs spread like lace across her chest. The hidden escapement clicked out a series of *ticks* and *tocks*, keeping time with her pulse.

In the center of the mechanism, slightly to the left, was a tiny hole encrusted with blood. Pearl inserted the key she kept on a chain around her neck and wound it clockwise until she felt a pinch of resistance in her breast. Then she scrubbed a tear from her cheek and yanked a pair of dark goggles down over her eyes. No sooner had she finished positioning them on her face, than the clocks in the shop came to life, *tick-tocking* and *coo-cooing*.

A second later, the first deep bellow of the Custom House Tower's eight o'clock shift vibrated through the walls, rattling the glass in the window and the pocket watches in the display case.

Pearl rasped out a quivering breath and clutched the arms of her work chair as reality split. With each strike of the bell, a fractured halo encircled her, visible only through the violet-lensed goggles she'd helped Dorian craft after the Break. They tinted her memories, shading each alternate circumstance with a different hue, helping her separate and sort them accordingly to provide a sliver of method with which to treat her madness.

Eight agonizing strikes of the bell later, and she finally had the courage to leave the letter she'd written Dorian on the corner of his worktable. She gathered up her suitcase and quietly slipped out of the Clockwork Apothecary, making her way to Tremont Street and across the Common. Toward the cast-iron fence that surrounded the Post Boston Infirmary and separated it from the rest of Late Boston.

Chapter Two

December 13ᵗʰ, 1916 – 8:33 a.m.

There were six timelines in all. As far as Isla could tell, she'd only died in one.

This fact brought her little comfort, seeing as how she was obliged to relive the incident four times daily. At seven o'clock in the morning and one o'clock in the afternoon. Then again at seven o'clock in the evening and one o'clock in the morning.

Thankfully, the laudanum helped her sleep through the worst of the late-night bells. Unfortunately, the tonic also ensured that she woke with one hell of a headache—made all the worse by the persistent, nightmarish tolling.

She stood at her hospital room window and squinted out over the city. The stark morning light forced its way through the clouds, gray with the promise of snow, and glared off the empty harbor in the distance.

Among the shadowy, squat buildings rose the slender column of the Custom House Tower with its infernal clock. Violet light seeped from its westward face and tinged the air with an unnatural glow, made all the more unsettling by the city's pallor. Isla's skin crawled, and her bones shuddered at the sight of it, but she'd committed herself to the chore of observing and documenting her recollections each waking hour. It was the only means she'd had of clinging to her sanity these past few months, cooped up in the unfinished west wing of the New State House that currently served as an infirmary for the more affluent victims of Late Boston.

Many of the patients were medicated around the clock and with heavier solutions than Isla had been pre-scribed. Dying more than once or twice had left them in a state of hysteria after the timelines converged. And dying more than that had left some comatose or worse.

Like her husband. Captain Leopold Le Guin.

At least, she *thought* he was her husband. She'd married him twice and had only called off the wedding once. The remaining three timelines left their union unsettled, with reality collapsing before the scheduled nuptials were to take place.

The uncertainty bothered her even more than the timeline in which she and the captain had been crushed to death under the bandstand in the Common whilst being photographed after the ceremony.

But it was the nine and three bells she dreaded most—according to the data she'd been keeping track of in her journal. There wasn't much else to do with her husband strapped inside an iron lung across the hall, hooked to all manner of tubes and machines. Her uncle's men, as well as the federal agents outside the quarantine fence, held the city captive. Her friend Mabel was in a morphine coma. And Captain Le Guin's mother and sisters weren't speaking to her. Not because of the timeline where she'd called off the wedding—she didn't think there had been enough time for them to discover that particular indiscretion—but because the man responsible for the machine that had caused the Break was none other than her father.

Guilty by association. That was just how the upper echelon operated. It was the reason Isla's uncle had encouraged her to use his last name when introducing her to his associates.

For all the grooming she'd received from Madam Pittard at *Institut de la Rose Raffinée*, learning how to socialize and dine with the gentry, how to talk and dress and host a party, her name was the one thing she had refused to change. The one thing her uncle couldn't *enhance,* no matter how many overpriced frocks or lessons he purchased.

Isla had been proud to be the daughter of the great Ezra Huxley. Even after her mother's accident, when her father had let her uncle ship her off to Switzerland so he could be alone with his grief and guilt. She'd believed he was only trying to spare her the weight of that misery. Now, here she was, trapped in an endless loop of suffering. And it was his doing. That was the saddest part of it all.

She had nothing to believe in anymore.

A knock echoed hollowly through the hospital room. Then the door opened wide, making way for Winifred McCaffrey and the large serving tray she balanced against the crook of one arm.

"You didn't join us for breakfast," she said accusingly.

Isla shrugged. "Seven o'clock hit harder than usual."

"Are you using the oxygen mask?"

"Only at night," Isla admitted, sure the nursing staff had already informed Winifred of her aversion to the apparatus. If she refused to put the mask on before turning in for the evening, they took the chore upon themselves after the laudanum knocked her out.

Isla closed her journal and moved it and a stack of books from the table in front of the window to a small desk in the corner, making room for the breakfast spread. Her appetite was lacking, but she knew better than to refuse her uncle's hospitality a second time.

"It's vital that you maintain your health, especially with winter settling in," Winifred lectured as she arranged saucers of bread, butter, cheese, and berries in front of Isla. "You've lost weight, and I'm not the only one who's noticed."

In the spaces between the dishes, she added silverware wrapped in a linen napkin, a poached egg on a pedestal, and a porcelain teacup that contained a thin layer of ground poppy. She filled the cup with water from a steaming kettle and added a splash of milk.

The meal was plainer than the breakfasts Isla had enjoyed at the finishing school but far richer than the stale oats her uncle's men rationed to the needier citizens. She watched them from her window every morning, huddled together outside the cast-iron fence that separated the haves from the have-nots. They spilled across Beacon Street and into the Common, waiting in long lines for the scraps her uncle allotted them.

It made Isla's insides boil and rot with guilt, but she refused to look away. Even when they begged for medical assistance that would never come. The infirmary only served Boston's Best. It seemed a silly distinction, considering the federal containment fence sliced through Beacon Hill, reaching all the way to the Charles River and trapping them every bit as effectively as the poor souls corralled on the other side of the city.

Winifred turned away to prop the empty breakfast

tray against the foot of the bed, giving Isla a glimpse of the braid coiled in a tight bun at the base of her neck. It was threaded with silver, and Isla wondered if it had been that way before the Break or if it were a new development. She studied the end of her own braid draped over her shoulder and tried to gauge whether the fiery luster had begun to seep from her locks. Was the weight of six timelines aging them prematurely?

"I know this is difficult, kitten, but it won't be long now," Winifred said, her lips pressing into an unconvincing smile as she buttered a slice of bread. Isla knew it was the best she could offer alongside such a lie. "One day soon, you'll be honeymooning in Paris with the captain, and all this will seem a distant dream."

"If there's anything left of Paris," Isla replied. She cradled the steaming teacup to warm her fingers. The radiator kept her room a comfortable temperature, but her hands were always cold. Madam Pittard had suggested it was due to poor circulation—as she'd tightened the laces of Isla's swan-bill corset.

Winifred cleared her throat, drawing Isla's attention away from the bleak view outside her window. She opened her hand toward the empty chair at the table, her expression growing more pained by the second. "Do you mind if I join you a moment?"

"By all means." The answer sounded terse, even to Isla's ears. After learning the woman had taken a position at her uncle's company, she'd been wary of her former governess. Of course, what was she to do after her only charge had set sail for Europe? A reference from the likes of Ezra Huxley wouldn't have gotten her very far in Boston. Besides that, Orwell had paid the tuition for her to finish medical school.

"Thank you." Winifred sat and adjusted the hem of her dark skirt before folding her hands in her lap. Her pensive stare prompted Isla to select a strawberry from the table. Perhaps she'd been tasked with not only delivering the breakfast but also confirming Isla consumed it.

Isla took a small bite, hoping the demonstration would appease Winifred and send her on her way. She washed it down with a sip of tea. The brew wasn't as bitter today, though it still made her wish for honey and a slice of lemon—or better yet, coffee. Though coffee wouldn't alleviate the throbbing in her temples.

"Sorry it's not stronger." Winifred nodded at the teacup.

"Are supplies growing thin?"

"No—well, yes, I suppose they are," Winifred amended. "But that's not the reason Mr. Orwell requested your dose be reduced this morning."

"He's punishing me for missing breakfast," Isla said flatly, unable to muster anger or even annoyance at the slight. It was another side effect of the opium tonics, one for which she was grateful. She didn't want to feel all the ugliness waiting for her on the other side of the drugs.

"No, not this time." Winifred wet her lips and attempted another uncomfortable smile. "Mr. Orwell believes that if he gains a better understanding of how the machine works, he might be able to reverse more than just the damage done to Boston."

"My uncle wants to win the war before it begins. I'm aware." Isla blinked slowly, wondering how this conversation would differ from the last two they'd had on the subject.

Winifred sighed. "You were there when he built the first model."

He. No one said her father's name aloud if they could avoid it. It was like a mud puddle they danced around for fear it would muck up their boots—or send them straight to hell. Even Winifred, who had once called Ezra Huxley the most brilliant man she'd ever met, now refused to speak his name.

Isla frowned. "I was fourteen and struggling through your algebra lessons. I can hardly remember the Pythagorean theorem, let alone equations required for time travel."

"He didn't detail his work when he wrote to you?" Winifred pressed. "No notes whatsoever about his later machines or their trials?"

Isla's gaze shifted back to the world beyond her window. "He didn't write to me at all. Not a single letter in five years." She took another gulp of tea, praying it would wash away the stain of rejection that darkened her mind.

"I'm sorry, kitten." Winifred pressed a hand over her heart. "I don't mean to keep putting you through this. I just thought that if you had something to offer Mr. Orwell, maybe he wouldn't…"

"Wouldn't what?" Isla asked, swirling the grainy residue in the bottom of her cup. "Why is he withholding medicine this time?" She was still convinced it was retribution for her not adhering to his strict agenda. Like the night she had missed the World Clock Council dinner, and he'd ordered the nurses to withhold her evening laudanum, letting her suffer through the late-night bells.

Somehow, Isla suspected that watching the surviving State House legislators lick her uncle's boots all evening would have been just as uncomfortable. It was disgraceful how easily they'd let him fearmonger them into disbanding and reforming as his useless committee of puppets, the oh-so-important-sounding *World Clock Council.*

But that was how Orwell worked. One way or another, he'd figure out what made a person tick. What they craved. Whether that be purpose or pleasure, distraction or drugs. Then he'd put them on a shelf and wait for the perfect opportunity to exploit the hell out of them.

Isla had just realized it too late.

"Finish your breakfast and make yourself presentable," Winifred said, her gaze sliding sideways and out the window. The purple light of the clock reflected off her eyes as a frown pinched her lips. "Your uncle has a favor to ask of you."

Chapter Three

December 13ᵗʰ, 1916 – 8:43 a.m.

Dorian didn't *hate* people. He just didn't like them very much. At least, not very many of them.

You either love the work or love the people you work for. That's what his ma used to say. She'd been a people person. A *people pleaser*, his pa had called her.

They'd been an ideal match. Dorian's pa loved working on clocks, and his ma loved finding the perfect one for every customer. He supposed it had been too much to hope that he'd inherit both of their abilities. Which was unfortunate, considering the work and the customers were now one and the same.

Pearl wasn't especially adept at pleasing people, either. But, like Dorian, she loved the work and was quite capable of tending to the Late Bostonians' needs. This allowed Dorian to focus on a more pressing task in the storeroom. They no longer needed the extra space for inventory. The timepieces they sold were one-of-a-kind and nonreturnable. Who would want to return a gear train necessary to jumpstart their heart or pump air into their lungs anyway?

Of course, the occasional repair came with the new territory. Dorian relied on Pearl for the brunt of that work, too. Which made the desperate banging at the front door all the more alarming.

"Pearl?" he shouted. When the pounding continued, he swore and removed the crystal he'd been faceting from the wet wheel of his lapidary table. It was nearly ready. But that would have to wait now until he figured out where his assistant had gotten off to.

He slipped off his headlamp equipped with its various jeweler's loupes and tinted lenses and wiped his hands on his waistcoat before rushing to answer the door. The store was dark except for the thin morning light filtering through the front window where two faces peered in at him, hands cupped around their eyes.

Mr. and Mrs. Messina, he recalled from their previous visits. They owned a bakery on the other side of Downtown Crossing.

Dorian twisted a knob on the wall, forgetting that the electricity had been shut off. He swore again and turned to the oil lamp on his worktable, turning the wick dial until fresh light spilled out, illuminating the display case. Then he cut across the room and unlocked the front door, opening it wide for the waiting couple.

"What can I do for y—?"

"It won't wind," Mrs. Messina said, grunting under her husband's weight as she readjusted his arm over her shoulder. Mr. Messina wheezed in protest. "He had a coughing fit last night, and now the damn ticker stem won't turn. He's been pale as a sheet since the eighth bell."

Mrs. Messina looked plenty pale herself, though that was in part due to the flour smeared across her cheeks and forehead. She and Mr. Messina were still in their kitchen aprons, the smell of bread yeast and molasses clinging to them the way gear oil and brass polish did to Dorian.

"He's probably just slipped a cog out of place. Let's have a look." Dorian took the man's opposite arm and helped his wife maneuver him into a wheelchair. From there, Dorian took over and pushed Mr. Messina behind the counter to sit alongside his worktable. An envelope with his name written across the front in Pearl's delicate handwriting caught his attention. He slipped it into his pocket for safekeeping and pulled on a magnifying visor, turning back to Mr. Messina.

The repair was simple and just as he'd predicted—a slipped cog. It was a common occurrence when melding machinery with biology. Dr. Doyle had warned that this could be a complication during the elementary medical lessons he'd given Dorian—shortly after helping him cut Pearl open to restart her heart.

The movements of the human body were not constant. Occasionally, lungs needed more air, and hearts required an extra tick or tock. The gear trains Dorian installed had to be flexible enough to accommodate the organic shifts but not so lenient that they fell out of sync anytime a person chuckled or sneezed.

Lots of customers had needed hinged braces for fractured bones after the Break, too. Dorian had fashioned spring-assisted joints and cogged hip sockets. All easy work. It was the inner cavity bits that he found most taxing. The skills required for those jobs were newer to his wheelhouse. Newer to everyone, he supposed.

Clockwork surgery. The innovative medical technique had been born out of necessity, and as such, there was a learning curve. And plenty of regular repairs to keep Pearl occupied while he obsessed over the machine taking shape in the storeroom.

"You might want to cut back on the cigarettes," Dorian advised as Mr. Messina exited the store with his wife tucked more comfortably against his side. The man smoothed his hand down the strap of his apron, subtly moving away from the bulge in his breast pocket.

"I'll sure try, Mr. Verne."

"Thank you," Mrs. Messina said for the fifth time. "Peter makes the lunch rounds before noon. I'll have him drop off something extra special for you and Miss Pearl. I know it's not much, but it's the best we can do for now."

"Lunch sounds wonderful." Dorian waved goodbye as they headed off down the sidewalk. He had an uneasy feeling about Pearl's letter. If it meant what he feared it might, preparing meals for himself wouldn't be among the worst of his troubles, but it would certainly be one of them.

At least the number of walk-ins had decreased in the last month. Dorian felt a twinge of shame as soon as the thought arrived. Not even he was ignorant or arrogant enough to believe that they'd saved all of Late Boston.

The Break had claimed its fair share of casualties. And then there were those who had died too many times to be helped for long. Dorian and Pearl did what they could, but with dwindling medical supplies and the compounding effects of the hourly bells…

More and more Late Bostonians lost themselves—their minds scrambled into oblivion by the ungovernable shifts of the time machine until they were nothing more than ghostly shells of themselves, wandering the city in search of a familiar place to die.

Dorian closed up the store and hung a sign in the window, promising to return before the eleventh bell. He preferred to be alone most hours of the day, but especially at nine and three. That timeline always wrecked him. He endured the striking of the bell locked in his bedroom, refusing to open the door for anyone—even Pearl.

Thinking of her reminded him again of the letter. He turned down the lamp at his worktable and retreated to the storeroom, fetching the envelope from his pocket. A crease had formed over one corner. Dorian tried to press it out with his fingers and instead smeared gear oil across the thick paper. It seemed the only errors he knew how to correct were mechanical in nature.

The longer he stared at the delicate lines and whorls of his name, the deeper the hooks of dread curled around his spine until he could take it no longer and ripped open the envelope.

Dearest Dorian,

History cannot be rewritten, and neither can it be forgotten. All that matters now is what we do with the time left to us. I've done all I can here with you, and others at the Post Boston Infirmary could benefit from clockwork surgery. That is where I've gone to offer my assistance. I pray you find peace in your heart and the strength to let go of the past.

With love,

Pearl

The letter crumpled between Dorian's shaking hands.

She was gone.

And not just to stay with Dr. Doyle for a night or two until her disappointment in him eased. She wasn't coming back this time. The seven o'clock bell had finally ruined them. *No.* Dorian was beyond that delusion. *He* had ruined them. It was just one more wrong he didn't know how to make right—that he *couldn't* make right. Not until the machine was complete.

He turned to face the opposite side of the room, where a wide metal hoop hung parallel to the wall. Purple crystals encrusted three-quarters of the device, strung together with copper wire. One of Ezra Huxley's journals lay on a stool Dorian had scavenged from the workshop ruins, the pages held open by a piece of raw quartz and an empty whiskey glass.

He'd tried to follow the diagram as closely as possible, but Dorian was no more a scientist than he was a surgeon. Clockwork had filled the gap for him in both regards. He just wasn't sure if it would be enough to get the job done this time.

Dorian plucked his father's watch from his waistcoat pocket and frowned at the minute hand as it pushed past eleven. He quickly tucked the timepiece away and exited the storeroom, locking the door behind him before taking the stairs up, two at a time.

Nine o'clock would have its way with him as it always did. But then he was determined to set aside self-pity and make another pilgrimage across Late Boston in search of purple crystals.

And hope.

Chapter Four

September 13th, 1916 – 7:23 a.m.

Before the morning was through, Isla would be a married woman.

She lay in bed and blinked up at the ceiling, mulling the idea in her mind as if anything could be done about it now. It felt too soon, even with her twentieth birthday approaching in a few short weeks. More than that, it felt *wrong*.

For one, it was the five-year anniversary of her mother's disappearance. Isla was sure that fact had not escaped her uncle, though she doubted he cared. But since he was footing the bill for the reception, she hadn't squabbled over the date. Time was of the essence, and Wednesdays were lucky. Still, how could she appreciate what was meant to be the happiest day of her life with the memory of the worst day pressing at the forefront of her mind?

And then there was the matter of love—or rather, the lackluster sentiments she harbored for her fiancé. He didn't inspire her to swoon or sigh the way Dorian Verne had any time his dark eyes sucked her in and threatened to swallow her whole. However, neither had anyone else since. Maybe she'd outgrown the capacity for such girlish feelings. The notion depressed her.

Isla guessed she could have rejected Captain Le Guin's proposal. But he was kind and handsome, and where would a refusal have left her? The finishing school was closing, thanks to the war pressing in on all sides, and with no word from her father, all that remained had been her tyrant of an uncle.

"Has the blushing begun?" Mabel Robida, Isla's dearest school friend, flopped onto the bed beside her and pulled the corner of the silk bedsheet over her head as if it were a bridal veil. "Is your belly swarming with butterflies yet?" she asked, an excited hitch in her voice.

Isla scoffed. "Does mild queasiness count?"

Mabel combed her hand through the waterfall of curls spread over Isla's pillow and clicked her tongue. "You look as pitiful as Ophelia, floating down her watery grave." Her fingers walked up Isla's arm and across her shoulder before tapping the underside of her chin. "Cheer up, Little Red. You can only be deflowered once, and I'm sure the captain will be gentle."

"No, it's not that—"

"So, you *don't* want him to be gentle, then? Perhaps a bit of spanking? Like the kind we read about in those novels old Pittard kept stashed in hat boxes under her bed."

"Mabs!" Isla's face burned at the memory, which only encouraged Mabel.

"Now *there's* a blushing bride." She grinned and threw the silk bedsheet back at Isla. "Let's get you dressed."

"I should really wait for Edith."

"Oh, yes." Mabel's shoulders squared, and her nose tilted upward. "A prop-*ah* lady does not exert herself with servantly duties," she recited in a nasal imitation of the English maid Isla's uncle had hired upon her return from Europe.

Isla wasn't fond of the woman, but after witnessing her uncle's harsh reprimand of a valet who had brought him the wrong morning coat, she didn't dare complain. Edith was good at her job—even if Isla suspected half of it entailed keeping her busy with an endless string of social functions. She'd been back in Boston for two whole months, and there were teas and luncheons and dinner parties every day. Her only reprieve had come when Mabel arrived for the wedding.

"Is that sausage I smell?" Mabel asked, her nose lifting higher. "Seems a bit early."

Isla nodded. "Breakfast is served with morning tea. Uncle likes to begin the workday early and doesn't care to be interrupted again until lunch."

"Barbaric," Mabel grumbled. "But no, you mustn't stoop to dressing yourself."

She slid off the bed and went to the French doors that led out to the balcony, pulling back the curtains to reveal the green and gold treetops of the garden across the street. Two rows of lavenders—purple glass panes Boston's Best had acquired in the last century—bookended the view, leftover from her uncle's latest remodeling project.

Mabel returned to the bed and touched Isla's cheek, misinterpreting her melancholy. "Soon, you can do whatever you like. Have elevenses at five in the morning or afternoon tea at midnight. You'll be mistress of your own house. Throw a party every week if you wish."

The idea put a lump in Isla's throat. The brownstone the captain had purchased in Back Bay would be easier to manage than the likes of her uncle's Beacon Hill mansion, but she had no intention of hosting parties. How could she entertain guests with her new husband dodging bullets on an airship over France?

Husband.

Isla had hardly wrapped her mind around the idea of having a fiancé. She hadn't expected to have a husband until sometime next year, or maybe after the war ended.

The wedding date had been pushed up since the captain's fleet enhancements were ahead of schedule—thanks to a generous contribution from Orwell Electric Laboratories. Soon, they would be ready to take their leave across the Atlantic and join the other American volunteers in the French Airforce.

Isla had the decency not to voice her resentment, and she was undoubtedly grateful that this meant she would be free of her uncle sooner rather than later. Unfashionably early breakfasts were the least of her qualms when it came to Abraham Orwell.

Her uncle's interference also saw her honeymoon downgraded from a month in Paris to a weekend in Pennsylvania. Though the destination wasn't entirely his fault, and the captain had promised to take her on a proper getaway after the war.

If he returned.

Her heart flopped miserably. It wasn't that she didn't *want* to love him, but news of the war and its casualties could be found everywhere one looked. The fighter pilots were especially vulnerable, and airships were slower and larger targets. Loving the captain almost certainly meant having her heart shattered when news of his demise arrived on her doorstep.

Isla tried to convince herself that this was the only

reason for her disquiet. It was merely a byproduct of poor timing and circumstances. And if—no, *when*—the captain returned, her affections would burst forth like a garden in spring, ripe for the plucking. The weight on her chest would lift, and she'd be free to give herself to her husband, and he to her. Completely. That girlish, besotted feeling she'd experienced with Dorian would return tenfold.

And once it did, perhaps then she'd be more inclined to indulge in those extracurricular activities from Madam Pittard's secret library.

Chapter Five

December 13th, 1916 – 9:34 a.m.

Abraham Orwell was not a patient man. It was a skill he'd struggled to hone his entire life. A virtue that lived and breathed in his mind, animated by his father's dying words.

All things come to those who wait.

And after all this time, Abraham still could not decide what his father had been waiting for. A cure for his mysterious illness? Or the welcome reprieve of death? Long before he'd fallen ill, the man had treated every aspect of his life as if it were an insufferable burden—including his occupation as a Harvard calculus professor, his soft-spoken wife, and their two healthy children.

When Abraham was a small boy, no more than six or seven years old, he'd dared to ask his father if he'd ever known happiness. The question had likely come after a scolding for playing too loudly or not buttoning his jacket properly. He could no longer remember, though his father's grim reply haunted him to this day.

God has seen fit to take away anything that ever brought me joy.

The words wounded Abraham anew as they sliced

through his memory, even with their edges dulled by time and context. His mother had lost four babies prior to his birth, and three more before his sister Elizabeth came along. After which, she became too frail to bear more children—or heartache.

Were he and Elizabeth things his father had waited for? Abraham wondered. Could that be enough to forgive the man for never finding joy in the company of his children? Enough to commit himself to his father's death mantra of patience?

Abraham could admit that, very often, his patience paid off. But, occasionally, life demanded a stronger hand. It was times such as these that he forgot patience and embodied his father's Victorian self-denial of joy instead, refusing to appreciate the finer things within his grasp. Loathing them, even. What good were they to him now? What good had they ever been?

He swallowed the last of his tea without tasting it and set aside the empty cup as he readjusted the telescope he'd had smuggled in from the Museum of Natural History. It had taken some time to procure the piece of equipment. Back Bay had survived the Break and was therefore not part of the clocked zone that was Late Boston.

Abraham's contacts feared not only being arrested

by federal agents outside the containment fence but also the possibility of being trapped inside during one of the hourly time warps that plagued the city. Luckily, he had enough scandal-worthy leverage to persuade them to comply with this small demand. Neither wall nor clock would stifle his influence.

Abraham squinted through the finderscope and angled the tube up past the crumbling apartment buildings until the Custom House Tower came into view. Then he moved to the eyepiece, taking a closer look at the marble and bronze clock with its glowing violet numbers. He searched the narrow windows to either side but detected no movement, only more of the unnatural light bleeding out above the city.

The men he'd tasked with entering the tower to investigate the machine further had returned with piss in their boots, blubbering on about phantoms and electrified nightmares come to life. Two of the men hadn't returned at all, and though the others claimed the machine had struck them down, Abraham knew defection was much more likely the cause.

Cowards.

His leg bumped the tripod, and the image on the lens blurred.

"Useless waste of time," he muttered to himself as

he twisted the focus knob.

A knock sounded at the office door, drawing him upright and away from the telescope.

"Yes?" His gruff, irritated voice was an echo of his father's. Most days, it sent a chill down his spine as if the man were reaching out and touching him from beyond the grave. But when he was in need of extra grit, the biological souvenir served as a whetstone for his ego.

Mr. Campbell, Abraham's secretary, cracked open the door and stuck his head inside the room. "Your niece is here, sir."

"Send her in," Abraham replied, turning back to the window that accommodated the telescope. He smoothed a hand over his beard and tried to focus his thoughts on the task at hand.

"You wanted to see me, Uncle?" Isla's voice was more delicate than Elizabeth's. It leaned dangerously close to her grandmother's, tugging at Abraham's heartstrings until it felt as if they'd snap and lacerate his lungs. He cleared his throat, buying a few extra seconds to compose himself before facing his niece. He could not afford to let nostalgia spoil his resolve. Not today.

Isla stood with her back to the closed door, hands folded over her navy-blue wool skirt. The garment was half of a walking suit Winifred had helped him pick out as a wedding gift. He wondered if Isla had chosen it to appeal to his kinder nature. Or maybe winter's reaching fingers had finally persuaded her to unearth the warmer clothing she'd packed in the bottom of the honeymoon luggage his men had retrieved from Captain Le Guin's recovered motorcar.

The rest of Isla's possessions had suffered the same fate as Abraham's, either looted or torched when riots swept through Beacon Hill in the early weeks after the Break. That's when he'd seized control of the State House.

"You weren't at breakfast this morning," Abraham said. Then, realizing how reprimanding the statement sounded, he added, "I hope you're feeling well."

"I have a mild headache," Isla admitted. "But I suppose that's to be expected with my dosage cut in half." Her voice was still honey and cream, though her words were laced with arsenic. She was Elizabeth's daughter, after all.

"Yes, well, I wanted your mind sharp for our conversation," he replied and waved his cane at the leather settees near the fireplace, inviting her to join him.

The senate president had been away on a family matter in Haverhill during the Break, and his east-facing office on the third floor presented the clearest view of that wretched clock. Commandeering the suite would have been an obvious move for Abraham, even without the generous mahogany and ornate décor. Or the gilded clock framed by wings that looked as if they belonged to the eagle head gripped in his fist.

And as the self-appointed President of the World Clock Council, he was entitled to a proper workspace. At least until he set the timeline right. After that, he didn't care which goldbrick they gave the room to. He'd own half the city.

"I've already told Dr. McCaffrey that I don't know anything about my father's latest endeavors," Isla announced as soon as she'd seated herself near the fire. "I wish I could be of more use—I truly do. Captain Le Guin and Mabel... It pains me to see them as they are. You must know that."

"Of course, of course," Abraham cooed to the best of his ability, his gravelly voice rolling out like the gentle warning of distant thunder. "But I believe there is another way you may yet prove useful."

"Oh?" Isla chewed her bottom lip. Her clasped hands twisted, wringing her fingers until the motion drew Abraham's scowling scrutiny. "How so?" she finally asked.

He reclined against the leather back of the settee and

laid his cane over his lap. She couldn't know how desperate he was. That wasn't how these games were won. "I've recently discovered that your childhood *friend*, Dorian Verne, has been poking around the old workshop, looting supplies and such for the clockwork remedies he's been peddling to the commoners."

Isla gasped. "Dorian? He's alive?"

Abraham cringed at her relief. He would have much preferred to let his niece believe the poor clocksmith had perished in the Break. The boy had shown up the day after Isla's return from Europe, sniffing around the estate like a street dog in search of a meal. It reminded Abraham of how Ezra had pursued Elizabeth, of how the unkempt inventor had reduced his sister to living in a grimy workshop loft, cooking meals and mending rags.

He'd be damned if he let the same fate befall Isla. And this time, he had the hindsight and resources to prevent it—though not before taking full advantage of the perversion that marred her formative years. Besides, this little hiccup would erase itself once he had control of the world clock.

"One of my men spotted Mr. Verne leaving the workshop with a satchel," Abraham continued. "I believe he may possess a journal that belonged to your father. One that might offer more details about the machine."

Isla cocked her head. "Then why not have your men retrieve it from him?"

Abraham blinked stiffly, taken aback by her forwardness. She knew him better than he cared to admit, but he had the good sense to feign offense at the suggestion.

"What sort of message would it send to Late Bostonians if the only medic at their disposal were approached with brute force?" He tsked. "No, no, my dear. That would not do at all."

"Hmmm." Isla's stare held fast, an annoyed tinge of discomfort pinching the outer corners of her eyes. "You're right, Uncle. The *commoners* don't need any more reason to eat the rich, do they?"

"There is also the risk that Mr. Verne might destroy the journal rather than turn it over to my men," Abraham added, ignoring the sardonic shift in her tone. "I hoped you'd be willing to offer a lighter touch."

"Me?" A flurry of emotions bloomed behind her eyes, progressing so quickly that Abraham struggled to appraise them.

She was certainly afraid. But of what? Going out among the mechanically modified masses? Being entrusted with such an essential assignment? Facing the scoundrel who'd hoped to undermine her future?

Isla was silent a moment longer, her emotions playing across her face as plainly as a motion picture, fear morphing into sorrow and then hope, anger, and defeat. The latter lingered as her attention once again settled on Abraham.

He sighed and reached over the narrow table between them to pat her tangled fingers. "Never you mind, dear. I should have known it was too tall an order—"

"I'll do it," Isla rasped, nearly choking on the words.

Annoyance curtailed Abraham's satisfaction. She was her father's daughter as much as her mother's. And, like Ezra, Isla was easily lured with visions of altruism and valor. While this made Abraham's current goal easier to manage, it unfortunately made the business of overseeing his niece's personal life vastly more complicated. She was too impressionable for her own good.

"Are you sure?" His hand curled over hers, warming the sharp, cold edges of her knuckles. "I understand if this is too much to ask."

"If it will help fix this mess, I'll do whatever it takes."

"Good girl." Abraham stood suddenly, the eagle-headed cane already gripped in his free hand. He crossed the room and pulled the door open wide. "Fetch my niece's walking coat and a hat, and call for Bradbury," he barked at Mr. Campbell.

"I'm to leave right now?" The color drained from Isla's face.

"The sooner, the better." He waved a hand at the gilded clock above the fireplace. "You could be back by luncheon, and then who knows? We might be home in time for dinner."

"Couldn't I have a cup of *tea* first?" Isla pleaded. Her fingers trembled as she lifted them to one side of her head.

There it was. The bait he'd been waiting for her to acknowledge. It worked so well, he considered keeping her in supply even after the timeline was righted.

"There will be plenty of tea waiting when you return," Abraham said, his voice dropping callously. "You must keep your wits about you if you're going into the city—and a watchful eye on the time. You know what one o'clock is like without your oxygen mask."

He resisted warning her of how dangerous the city could be for an unattended young lady, especially a city that had fallen on such hard times as theirs. She looked grave enough. Besides, it was the middle of the day, and plainclothes officers were stationed downtown.

Isla's thirst for opium would surely keep her on task, Abraham decided, shrugging off the guilt that had begun to creep over him.

"I've Mrs. Le Guin's traveling attire, sir," Mr. Campbell called from the outer office. "And Mr. Bradbury is waiting."

"Very well." Abraham turned back to Isla as she stood. "Off you are, my dear."

"That was fast." Her mouth fell open and closed again, her brows puckering as confusion melted into grim understanding. There had never been a choice for her to make. This conversation was merely a courtesy. A formality.

"Three hours." Abraham stamped the end of his cane on the floor to hurry her along. "That should be plenty of time."

"I-I'll do my best," Isla stammered. She made for the door and let out a little gasp as his cane cut her off.

"I know you will." He leveled a meaningful stare at his niece, waiting for her gaze to meet his one last time. "The captain and Miss Robida are counting on you. And supplies are running low."

Isla swallowed and inched past the doorway as soon as he lowered the cane. She took her coat and hat from Mr. Campbell and followed Bradbury without another word.

She would return with the journal. Abraham was sure of it.

He bit down on the fleshy inner walls of his cheeks, denying the smirk that twitched behind his lips. It was too meager a victory to yield to joy just yet. And now he was forced to retreat into the bitter embrace of patience, whispering through his mind like the wind as it stripped the last leaves of autumn from their branches.

Chapter Six

December 13th, 1916 — 9:44 a.m.

The Huxley workshop hadn't been much to look at before the Break, but the earthquakes had done it no favors. If Dorian were perfectly honest, the place had never recovered after the incident with Mrs. Huxley.

A single snowflake drifted past the gaping hole in the ceiling, melting as it landed on his cheek. He wiped the spot of moisture away and frowned up at the dark clouds impeding his search. Glass teeth lined the section of rusty atrium framework that had endured the onslaught of time and turmoil, though it offered little protection from the icy breath of winter that wove through upended tables and mangled machinery, ripping splinters from the floor and stirring scraps of brittle paper and dead leaves. This lighter plunder was winnowed into a blackened corner of the building, slick with soot from a fire Dorian was still unconvinced had been an accident.

He paused to stretch his back and closed his eyes, trying to remember what the workshop had been like five years ago, but all he could picture was Isla's face. Her glowing, amber-hued gaze. The crease that split the swell of her bottom lip on the rare occasion she wasn't grinning ear to ear. The flush that tinted her cheeks any-time she turned to find him walking through the door.

Some nights, when Dorian was feeling especially sentimental—usually after a pint too many at the local tavern—he found himself sitting on the edge of the loft landing. Boots dangling over the remains of the tinkering floor, strewn with broken dreams and shattered atrium glass.

But today, he was sober, and his time was better spent wading through the debris in search of oraclyst.

Ezra had fittingly named the purple quartz by blend-ing the words *oracle* and *amethyst*. He'd explained this decision to Dorian as they trudged through a collapsed section of an abandoned subway tunnel under the city, where Ezra had discovered another cache of crystals. Stories of the temple in Delphi, where the most famous of the ancient world's prophets had lived, helped to pass the time as they'd toiled in the damp and dark, harvesting oraclyst by the light of lanterns and mining helmets.

It was unfortunate that the bulk of that labor resided in the Custom House Tower, fueling the machine Ezra had tied to the new clock and its excruciating bells. But Dorian had deciphered enough of the inventor's mad ramblings and scrawling hand to understand that only a single loop was required. Not the six that filled the tower.

And while the few subway headhouses that had survived the Break were either boarded up or guarded, Ezra had left the original machine intact at the workshop. Even after he'd lost hope of Elizabeth using it to return to him.

Of course, like the rest of the city, it had not fared well in the Break. The electrified rods used to elevate the portal ring had rattled free from their footings, and much of the crystal had shattered into unusable fragments, now strewn across the shop floor. Dorian had recovered the largest of the surviving pieces two months ago, though it hadn't been enough to construct a new quartz ring—not even at a third of the original scale.

So, back to the workshop he went in search of more.

At first, it had been a weekly outing. But lately, he found himself returning every day and night, foraging through the ruins and memories, hoping he might one day make sense of both.

And then, just maybe, he would be worthy of her.

His very own oracle.

Isla.

Chapter Seven

September 13ᵗʰ, 1916 – 6:41 a.m.

A horn blasted, sending Dorian's pulse punching at his temples as he darted between a motorcar and a trolley. He ignored the slurs the drivers shouted at him and hunted for an opening in the foot traffic that filled the sidewalk.

Downtown Crossing swarmed with mill workers and schoolboys, businessmen and shoppers, all dressed in dark coats and hats, turning the city into a giant anthill. Dorian fell into step alongside them. This was his colony, after all. Boston was home, for better or worse.

Familiar faces peeked through the crowd, and people shouted casual greetings back and forth. The handle of an umbrella cracked Dorian's elbow as he cut around an elderly lady taking her time. He snarled in protest, but then the street clock on the corner up ahead came into view, drawing a groan from him that the early-morning clamor smothered.

He was running late. What was new?

The timepiece he'd inherited from his father felt like a lead weight in his pocket, silently mocking him. He'd refused to wind it after the funeral. As if that would somehow slow time until he had a chance to catch his breath.

Life was coming at him much too quickly. The future unfurled in his mind like a mainspring lashing out of its barrel, only he couldn't roll this one up and put it back in its rightful place.

Isla was getting married.

Today.

In a few hours' time.

To someone who was not him.

Despite the unrelenting march of time, Dorian's gaze snagged on a window display before he'd reached Milk Street. He slipped free of the bustling horde and pressed his face near the glass, taking in the rows of delicate silver bands dripping with floral filigree. Sapphires, rubies, and diamonds sprouted from their pronged settings, glittering under the store lights and a sign promoting their big bridal sale.

Now's your chance! Let forever begin today!

Dorian snorted and shook his head. If only he'd stowed away on the ship that had taken Isla off to Europe. Or found out sooner that she'd returned. Or had the nerve to darken her uncle's stoop a moment longer, refusing to leave until she came to the door.

No, there were no more chances left for him.

The wedding invitation had been like an arrow through the foot, pinning him in place. How could he continue pursuing Isla when she was promised to another? It would have been inappropriate. Scandalous, even.

He'd done his best to put the idea out of his mind, but it was no use. The thought of eloping with Isla as if they were characters in some Shakespearian tragedy burned him alive every waking moment, granting no reprieve as the days spun out of control. And now, here he was. Bitterly considering engagement rings in the eleventh hour.

Pathetic.

Dorian's gaze slid away from the window and up to the street clock again. He swore under his breath and joined the marching ants on the sidewalk once more, making his way to State Street where he turned right and headed for the Custom House.

The building's new tower cut a thick shadow through the sunrise crawling up from the harbor. It loomed over the city like a king lost on a chessboard. The addition had been completed early last year, but the clock had taken a bit longer—especially after the job had been turned over to Ezra Huxley.

Dorian was more than a little hurt that Ezra had not

requested his assistance. Clockwork was his bread and butter, after all. But then again, they hadn't parted on the best terms after the inventor's latest time machine trial left Dorian with scorched fingers and his hair on end.

Dorian had been too infuriated to bite his tongue. He'd hurled a few choice words at Ezra that he *mostly* regretted now. So, when Ezra invited him to inspect his work in the tower that morning, he'd agreed. It was time to clear the slate.

Dorian climbed the front steps and entered the building, crossing the lobby to join the wait for an elevator. After the brisk walk, he was too winded for that many stairs. At the nineteenth floor, he exited and loaded into another elevator to complete the journey.

As the doors slid open on the twenty-fourth floor, Ezra greeted Dorian with a manic smile, cheeks swollen and smeared with gear oil. More streaked his graying hair, whipping it into stiff peaks.

"Why did the scientist drop a wristwatch into his flask?" he asked, standing as tall and proud as the Mad Hatter.

"Because the doctor told him to watch his drinking?" Dorian guessed with a shrug.

"Oh, that's good!" Ezra chuckled. "Good, but wrong. He was looking for a timely solution. Which I think I've found," he added, pressing a finger to the side of his nose.

"What?" Dorian's breath wheezed nervously. Try as he might, he always got excited when Ezra looked this way, eyes aglow with unraveling secrets. His euphoria was contagious. No matter how many times it ended in failure and mild electrocution.

The past five years had been full of enough false alarms that Dorian knew better than to get his hopes up. And today of all days was not the time to get swept away in a would-be breakthrough.

"Isla's wedding is in three hours," he reminded Ezra as he followed him into the mechanical room. "You need to be there to walk her down the aisle."

"I can do one better than that." Ezra stopped in front of the raised platform that held the inner workings of the clock. A series of gears formed the going train that regulated the time displayed on all four faces of the tower. It was a larger scale than Dorian was accustomed to, but he understood how it worked.

Chains ran from the gear train's larger wheels, reaching for the back wall where a massive copper barrel punched with square holes rested on a second platform. The landing was attached to the first by a narrow walkway made of old boards. Above the drum stretched a loom of cables that fed through an opening in the ceiling, disappearing into the belfry.

The design was larger and more complex than the original, which had called for an undersized winding motor and no bells at all. But Ezra was old friends with the architect of the tower, and he'd landed the job by promising to make the city dance with customizable tunes hammered out on dozens of bronze bells—a carillon that crooned as effortlessly as a pianola. Those plans had significantly increased the clock's budget, which didn't seem to faze Ezra, though it terrified Dorian on his behalf.

Even angry, Dorian had stopped by to check on Isla's father at the workshop, but it had been Dr. Doyle who'd solved the mystery of the inventor's disappearance, recounting the details of Ezra's grand plans for the new clock that he'd shared during a house call—a *Custom House* call—to treat a persistent case of the sniffles.

If the clock failed to impress, Ezra would be ruined. He was hanging by a thread as it was, living in the tower where he worked since the lights and water had been shut off at the workshop, and foreclosure notices papered the front door. The only possessions he'd taken with him were his journals—and, apparently, a hefty supply of crystals.

Six glowing rings of violet quartz boxed in the open space beneath the gear platform. Four sides, a top, and a bottom. Inside the cube, slightly to the left, swung a long pendulum. To the right hung a caged stack of cast-iron weights with crystal corner pieces.

Given Ezra's knowledge of electricity and his fanatical admiration of Edison and Tesla, Dorian was still confused as to why he had designed the clock to be wound manually. But even more perplexing were the electrical components he *had* employed.

Copper wires spiraled up the four legs of the platform, crisscrossing like a lattice along the underside and reaching down the length of the pendulum, which Dorian now realized was a dry cell battery. The wires also wrapped around the chain attached to the weights before linking into one of the quartz portals.

"What is all this?" Dorian demanded, his pulse now pounding in his ears. "I thought you'd given the time travel experiments a rest."

"Yes, yes," Ezra grumbled. "Well, mostly."

"Mostly, you say?" Dorian huffed and turned as if to retreat to the elevator. But then, thinking of Isla, he clenched his teeth and spun back around. "I will not attend a wedding with my hair looking like a porcupine's. If you called me here to be a test subject—"

"Oh, no, no, no." Ezra waved his hands. "There's no need for that—I stayed up all last night testing the machine. It works marvelously."

"I see," Dorian said, though he most definitely did not see. "If you no longer needed my assistance, and this new machine works so well, why didn't you travel back to yesterday and cancel our meeting?"

Ezra chuckled. "Well, that's not quite how this one works. See here…" He pointed out the crystal portals as if Dorian had somehow missed them. "I can only seem to get an hour's worth of history out of each one of these—that is, if I don't want to knock out power for all of Boston. And I promised Peabody that I'd manage the clock without tapping into the building's electricity."

"Hence the dry cell," Dorian said, nodding to the battery pendulum.

"Reducing future expenses was the only way to justify the added cost of the bells," Ezra continued. "By enclosing the rings around the weights and pendulum, I've created an electromagnetic field that essentially *rewinds time* every six hours."

"It lifts the weights?"

"It returns them to their position six hours prior."

"And recharges the battery, too?" Dorian asked, his bewilderment growing.

"Yes," Ezra confirmed.

"A true design of perpetual motion. Incredible!" Dorian circled the platform, his interest peaking despite his resistance. "And you tested this? Last night?"

"I did." Ezra's emphatic pride dwindled into something humbler and more practical than Dorian was used to. But it peaked once more as he glanced down at the watch pinned to a buttonhole in his waistcoat. "Here, here!" he whispered, waving a finger at the machine. "This is the first hour I've linked with the main bell. Have a listen."

Dorian felt his teeth rattle in his skull as the first knell of the bell struck him like a tuning fork. He slapped his hands over his ears and watched the glowing crystal portals begin to pulse. Crackling arcs of electricity leapt from the pendulum bob to the hanging weights, turning the inside of the cube bright blue. Each resounding toll sent a surge of adrenaline through Dorian's veins, quickening his blood until his heart was giddy with it.

"Did you accomplish anything of note with your six rewound hours?" he asked as soon as the bell had finished its chore.

"Well, no," Ezra admitted. "You see, it doesn't work that way. It winds the clock, reversing time for the driving mechanism alone. I've even isolated it from the going train so that it doesn't affect the time indication."

"But shouldn't the electromagnetic field work for anything—any*one* within its range?" Dorian stammered, on the verge of volunteering for another trial even after outright refusing only a moment before. The narrow space between the swinging pendulum and the hanging weights looked wide enough to fit a man. One brave enough to risk the blue lightning the machine produced, anyway.

Ezra sighed, but the sound was more resolved than disappointed. "I had hoped as much, but if my late-night trials did somehow send me back in time, I'm afraid they dragged my memory along for the ride. It's a bit difficult to make good use of stolen time once you've forgotten how you spent it the first go-around."

"So…you need a second pair of eyes to observe the phenomenon?"

"Perhaps." Ezra cocked his head from side to side. "But not today, my good sir."

"Right! No. Of course not." Dorian cleared his throat and took a step back from the contraption, blinking as if waking from a dream. "It's a great achievement, regardless. A wonderfully productive use of oraclyst and your research."

"It is, isn't it?" A lopsided grin brightened Ezra's

face. "And, best of all, the carillon tumbler arrived yesterday." He waved a hand at the copper drum behind the gear platform. "I've set the bells to play Isla's favorite song—or at least it *was* her favorite song—at noon, when they make their honeymoon getaway."

"I'm sure she'll love it." Dorian turned his back to the machine, pushing all the possibilities into one corner of his mind. Another trial could wait. There'd be time for all that after Isla finished cutting out his heart and feeding it to the birds.

"You need a bath," he noted, taking in Ezra's appearance a second time.

"Yes, of course."

"And a proper suit." Another twinge of guilt struck Dorian. He wished he had mended their rift sooner and had more time to help Ezra prepare for today. But, since the new machine wasn't *that* kind of machine, they would have to make do with the few hours they had before the wedding.

"Don't you worry about me, Mr. Verne." Ezra slapped his shoulder, then made an about-face as he attempted to wipe away a bit of grease he'd left behind on Dorian's sleeve.

"You're sure you don't need my help?" Dorian pressed, taking inventory of the oil slicks on Ezra's clothes and the stains on his hands and forearms. "I could loan you a three-piece. Polish your shoes. Rob a soap truck," he offered.

"I've got money enough for a suit and soap," Ezra huffed. "And I'll have plenty more once the clock impresses Boston's Best this afternoon." He shooed Dorian off toward the elevator. "Go have breakfast with Pearl. I'll see you at the Common for the ceremony."

The ceremony.

Dorian's stomach knotted, but he managed a weak smile for Ezra's sake.

"Have you seen her yet?" Ezra asked. "Since she returned?"

"No," Dorian confessed. "She's been very busy." The excuse tasted like vinegar in his mouth. He wanted to spit it out, but the only other option was that she didn't want to see him. And that couldn't be. She'd sent him an invitation, after all.

"Naturally," Ezra said, nodding to himself. "I've been busy, too."

"You haven't seen her, either?" Dorian's forced cheer wavered, but only for a second. They both had more doubt and regret than they knew what to do with. Best not to feed it. "She's going to be so thrilled to see you."

"And you, as well." Ezra mirrored his tight smile. "It will be a happy day."

"The happiest," Dorian agreed, his gaze following the inventor's back to the clock's curious inner workings and its amethyst glow. "One to remember for all time."

Chapter Eight

December 13th, 1916 – 10:05 a.m.

The Common was quiet. It always was just before and right after the world clock announced the hour and rearranged everyone's memories of Isla's wedding day.

The tolling didn't seem to bother Bradbury, but then again, not everyone's schedules had been as deeply altered by the Break as those closest to her—or to her father, rather. Or those who had died in multiple timelines. Isla was just grateful that Bradbury had let her catch her breath after the ten o'clock bell before rushing her out into the freezing clutches of December.

She pressed one hand over her felt tricorne hat to keep the wind from blowing it off her head and followed her uncle's henchman past the bronze General Hooker sculpture in front of the infirmary's west wing.

Despite the cold, it felt good to breathe fresh air again. Her eyes watered from the stiff wind, and her nose was numb by the time they reached the cast-iron fence that ran along Beacon Street. Bradbury dug a cigarette from the breast pocket of his coat. He clamped it between his lips and rattled a box of matches while two guards set to work unlocking the gate.

Isla couldn't help but stare at the rifles slung across the men's backs, the stocks sliding soundlessly over their long, black coats. From her hospital room window, they'd looked like tiny debonair soldiers in their bowler hats. They were less charming up close with their hostility in sharp focus.

As they pulled the gate open, their gazes searched the shadows of the nearby buildings. Isla realized Bradbury was doing the same, even as he cupped his hands to light his roll-up. They were more concerned with people trying to get inside the infirmary than with her release.

Release.

As if she were being let out of prison. The idea would have been comical if it weren't so depressingly close to the truth. She had a sudden urge to tear off down Park Street. Just in case Orwell changed his mind and ordered them to drag her back to her room, kicking and screaming. But he'd already given her enough incentive to return.

The captain and Miss Robida are counting on you.

The medical intervention her maybe-husband and best friend required was a deal more involved than the teas and laudanum Isla relied on. And Orwell had already proven he was not above a little torture to get his way— not even with family. But if Isla didn't come back with her father's journal, she knew she wouldn't be the only one who suffered for it.

"This is where I get off," Bradbury said, touching the brim of his derby hat. Smoke curled up from his nostrils and outlined the crooked bridge of his nose. "But don't you worry. Your uncle has eyes all over the city. You need any help, you just holler."

Isla swallowed and managed a small nod before slipping past the guards. But as the gate closed behind her, she wondered. Would she need help? How long would a well-to-do lady in a fancy walking suit take to draw unwelcome attention in the trenches of Late Boston?

If she hurried, maybe she wouldn't have to find out.

She clutched the collar of her coat tighter around her neck and crossed the street, her heels clicking as she stepped up onto the sidewalk and took cover in the broken shadows of the trees bordering the Common. Her mind raced, throbbing with each step, but she continued onward.

The steeple of the Park Street Church peeked through the naked branches overhead. It was a familiar landmark that helped Isla recall the route she'd taken through downtown with her mother, running household errands.

The butcher, the baker, and the doohickey makers, she'd

sung, skipping to keep up with her mother's sweeping gait. A pace she now felt burning in her legs as she neared Tremont Street.

She tried to remember the places they'd visited less frequently. The stores that sold tools and supplies for her father's work. Or strange new gadgets for the kitchen, like toasters and coffeemakers. Dress boutiques for the rare ballet outing. And watches for when her father deconstructed his to use the parts in one of his inventions.

Temple Place. That was where she needed to go. Isla cut right and passed the boarded-up entrance to Park Street Station. A block later, she turned left. Her feet ached already, and she cursed her heeled boots for being more fashionable than practical. But she was nearly there.

The Clockwork Apothecary was just as she remembered, sandwiched between two pillar-laden Greek revivals. A wide, half-moon window stretched high above the storefront, its white trim bold against red brick. It had always reminded Isla of a clock face, peeking out at the customers below as they *oohed* and *ahhed* over the lovelies in the window.

Of course, the display was empty now. She supposed it had been for some time. None of the stores would have received new shipments since the Break. Isla tried the handle of the door before noticing the *Closed* sign. A paper clock with faux dials indicated that someone would return by eleven.

She tried the door again, then tapped her knuckles against the glass and pressed her face against it to peer inside. A grandfather clock in the corner revealed it was only a quarter after ten. Waiting that long was not an option, she realized as the reflection of a man in the store window caught her eye.

He lingered in the shadow of a building across the street, a paperboy cap pulled down low on his forehead. His jacket was patched in the elbows, and when he unfolded his arms and started toward her, she noticed the handle of a pistol sticking out of his waistband.

Isla didn't run. At least, not until she reached Washington Street. She rounded the corner and tore off toward Downtown Crossing. As a girl, it had been a crowded, noisy area with a police officer always within arm's reach. Now, the department stores were quiet, their doors locked tight and windows dark. Only a handful of people loitered on the sidewalks, and none of them had a friendly look to spare.

Isla's breath pinched in her chest as her stride stalled, and she coughed into the bend of her elbow. She stole a glance over her shoulder, back the way she'd come. The man hadn't followed—or if he had, he was doing a better job of hiding it.

She straightened and tried to breathe through her nose. Her heart still hammered out a warning, but she feared it had more to do with the personal demons fueling her quest than the idea of being mugged in the street. An invisible icepick chipped at her brain, and salty sweat slicked her upper lip despite the cold.

She wondered if the Oriental Teashop in Scollay Square carried a brand that might remedy her. If they were still open. Or had the giant golden kettle on their sign run out of steam? She certainly was.

But onward she journeyed.

Past the Old South Meeting House and the Old State House, catching glimpses of the looming violet clock at intersections and in between the buildings as she went.

Isla was panting by the time she reached the statue of Samuel Adams with his folded arms and rueful glare directed at the spot where the Adam's Square subway headhouse had once been. The baroque structure and its lovely clock had been swallowed by a large crack that'd split open Washington Street and ran north.

Isla leaned against the base of Adam's monument to catch her breath, propping herself against a slope of granite beneath an inscription that read: *A statesman,*

Only because he never met my uncle, she thought, forcing herself upright once more. She was nearly there. She couldn't give up now. But unlike the bronze rendering of Adams, Isla was made of flesh and blood—blood that seemed to be rushing to her head at the moment.

More people were on the streets now, bustling about with whatever errands they could still manage between the hours. Some shuffled slowly as if sleepwalking, eyes glassy and vacant. Others glared at her new walking suit and hat, their threadbare garments coming apart at the seams. But Isla had the good sense to realize that they had likely been in this state long before the Break. It didn't make her feel any better. Nor any safer.

A carriage lumbered by, its horses gaunt and needing to be reshod. Several motorcars were parked along the curb, as well, though Isla didn't suspect they'd venture far with missing tires and dissected motors. A pair of men hunkered over one of the mechanical carcasses paused to stare as she passed, their narrowed gazes daring her to challenge them.

Isla looked away. Her heels clicked more fiercely on the cobblestone as she cut through Dock Square and turned up North Street. She wouldn't find any of the wealthy socialites her uncle had encouraged her to befriend out and about on this side of the city. Most of Boston's Best had even abandoned their homes in favor of the security the Post Boston Infirmary offered. Those who didn't require treatment were accommodated in the east wing.

Orwell only had so many guards at his disposal. He couldn't afford to station one at every house in Beacon Hill. But he'd promised that once the timeline had been corrected, the federal government would help fund the city's reconstruction, including any loss of personal property or damages. He'd promised order would be restored.

But order for whom? Isla wondered, taking in the bitter poverty that had sunk its teeth into Boston.

It was no secret that her uncle only catered to those who could somehow serve a purpose. Even Isla wasn't so foolish as to believe the man spoiled her out of the goodness of his heart. Especially not after his immediate interest in Captain Le Guin's airship unit once their engagement had been announced.

"It's too cold, Mama." A crying child drew Isla's attention near Merchant's Row. The young mother dragging the girl along stripped off her shawl and wrapped it around her daughter's shoulders, knotting it under her chin.

"There, you see?" she said with brittle cheer. "All better."

"I'm tired," the child wailed.

"Me, too." The mother sighed, but then clenched her teeth as a stiff wind whipped her hair and the hem of her skirt. "Let's find some food, and then we can go home," she said, standing up straight as she noticed Isla. Her gaze dropped sullenly to the navy walking suit.

Before Isla knew what she was doing, she'd unbuttoned her coat and handed it over.

"Take it, please," she said as the woman flinched away from her. "I'm almost home."

And she was. The Huxley Workshop waited up ahead. At the corner of North and Blackstone. She could see it now. The broken atrium ceiling glistened in the gray sunlight filtering through the clouds.

The woman snatched the coat from her hands and skipped back a few steps before tugging it on.

"Thank you," she said, biting off the word as if she begrudged the gift but was too desperate to refuse it. Isla knew that feeling all too well. Her gratitude had been uttered with just as much resentment when *she* had accepted the suit from her uncle.

The mother and daughter hurried off toward Faneuil Hall, their gazes flicking up briefly at the purple aura of the world clock beyond. Isla did the same.

Thirty minutes until the next bell, she noted, hugging herself in an attempt to still the shivers that racked her shoulders. Lace blouses were fine for indoor teas, but they were useless out in the wintery elements. She felt exposed, and the sensation only intensified with the hungry gazes that traced her path through downtown.

Her boots set to work again, faster yet, and her mind scrambled to formulate a plan that didn't include getting mugged or freezing to death. She wondered how her mother's wardrobe had fared. Had her father packed up and shipped off what was left of her, too? Or could he not be bothered, too lost in his diabolical machinations? The idea of either depressed Isla, but at least the latter might yield a coat for the trip back to the infirmary.

Maybe she'd even find her father's journal. Her thoughts swelled with more potent hope.

There was a chance that Dorian had overlooked it in favor of more useful tools and supplies. Food and clothing. She clung to that possibility, taking comfort in its safety. Because Dorian knew exactly how to derail her life—how to unmoor her like a hot air balloon without a prayer of safely landing.

She'd already let him once. Nearly twice, though she couldn't be certain. But one thing she was sure of was that it couldn't happen again. She was a married woman now, and lives were at stake. If the journal held the solution to fixing the timeline, then the entire city depended on her. There was no time for stoking old flames.

And there was no need.

Not when the Break had turned her heart to ash.

Chapter Nine

December 13th, 1916 – 10:35 a.m.

Dorian hadn't expected to find more than a lump or two of crystal. He'd been picking the workshop over for months. Still, it disappointed him to leave with his satchel so light, and his heart so heavy.

On his way out, his boots dragged across the floor, toes searching the shadows and rubble for anything he might have missed. Just as he reached the vestibule, someone wrenched the front door open. The rusty hinges squealed out a warning that made him yearn for the tinkling bells that had greeted him as a child. They'd been stolen a month earlier, likely smashed in the Common with so many others in a demonstration of the Late Bostonians' unrest.

Dorian had encountered more than a few vandals on his excursions to the workshop. He'd even earned a decent knife wound for his trouble. After which, he'd dug through his father's possessions and found the old flintlock pistol passed down from his great-greatgrandfather, who had fought in the Revolution. He kept it tucked in his waistband for safety's sake, though he wasn't entirely sure if he'd loaded it correctly.

He hoped he wouldn't have to find out as he watched a dark silhouette slip past the threshold. A woman, he realized from the outline of her skirt.

"Who's there?" she called, sensing him in a shadowy corner of the tinkering floor. "Father? Is that you?" She shifted, and sunlight haloed her tricorne hat, lighting the bound curls beneath on fire.

"Isla?" Dorian couldn't believe his eyes. He blinked stiffly and took a careful step toward her, fearing his mind was playing tricks on him, and she might disappear if he moved too suddenly—or bolt like a spooked dove. But he should have known she wouldn't scare so easily.

"What are you doing here?" she demanded, her voice laced with a snarl.

"What am *I* doing here?" Dorian echoed. "What are *you* doing here?"

"This is my father's workshop." Isla lifted her chin and grabbed her hips with both hands, looking every bit her mother. "And I asked you first," she added, sounding more like the stubborn girl he'd known not so long ago. Her attention dropped to the satchel at his side. "What are you stealing there?"

"Stealing?" Dorian's shoulders squared. "Nothing anyone else wants, I can assure you that."

"Can you?" Isla huffed and stalked past him, taking

to the rickety loft stairs. She reached for the railing, but then, noting the rust and jagged edges, lifted the hem of her skirt instead. She navigated the steps carefully in her fancy boots.

"Where are you going?" Dorian shouted after her.

"Again, Mr. Verne, this is my father's workshop," Isla said with an irritated sigh. "I don't owe you any explanation. But, if you must know, I'm in need of a coat."

He snorted and rested his arm on the wobbly post at the base of the stairs. "Did you suppose that silly hat would keep you warm enough?"

No sooner had the words left his mouth, than the stiff felt smacked him square in the face. The black ostrich feather tucked in the brim tickled his nostrils, and downy tendrils stuck to his lips. He sputtered and spat them out before loosing a sneeze.

"I bought it because it reminded me of *you* and the *ridiculous* games you used to play." Isla glared down at him, teeth clenched and nostrils flaring. "And you're one to talk, wearing those purple goggles."

"We," Dorian said just as rigidly. "The ridiculous games that *we* used to play."

"I hated those stupid games." Isla's bottom lip quivered, and her eyes glassed over as if she might cry. "And I hate you." She turned away from him and continued up to the loft.

"Lies!" Dorian scooped up the discarded hat and chased after her, taking the stairs two at a time. Isla had already disappeared through the arched opening, but she couldn't go far. "You loved those games. You *begged* for them."

"Only because my parents were too poor to take me to the opera or ballet," she shouted back. "That's where I should have been—not traipsing around a workshop with a clocksmith's son."

"Ezra took you to the ballet."

"Twice." Isla scoffed. "Swan Lake. It was the only one I'd seen before Europe. I was the laughingstock of my school."

Dorian cut through the small kitchen with its pot-belly stove and farmhouse sink, following the sound of Isla's voice. He found her in her parents' bedroom, hunched over a large trunk that he was sure had been riffled through by at least a dozen homeless people at this point.

"My deepest apologies," he said, dipping into a mocking bow. "I had no idea you found my company so lacking. Fetch me some tights, and I'll make it up to you."

"Don't be absurd." Isla sighed and crumpled to the

floor, her wool skirt folding behind her legs. She held up a laced leather corset vest and a moth-eaten shawl trimmed with fur.

"You're right. I've got two left feet. I guess I could give opera a go." He plopped her girly pirate hat on his head, nestling it down on top of his goggles, and cleared his throat as if preparing to belt out a tune.

"It's too late, Dorian."

"Nonsense. I'm not an old dog yet. I'm sure there's a trick or two left in me."

"I mean, it's too late for us." She dropped the foraged garments onto her lap and looked up at him. Her eyes were bloodshot and rimmed with shadows. He'd been so caught up in seeing her again, in their perilous and precious banter that fed his soul, that he'd forgotten she hadn't answered his question.

"Why *are* you here?" he asked, more gently this time.

Isla tore her gaze away from his and picked at a knot in the vest's laces. "My uncle asked me to retrieve a journal that belonged to my father. He thinks it may hold the solution to righting the timeline." She looked at Dorian again, brows knitting with suspicion. "You wouldn't know anything about it, would you?"

"About what? A journal?" Dorian had never been a gambling man, and it was a good thing because he'd been told his poker face looked as if he'd just been caught pissing on the Boston Stone. It wasn't fooling Isla either.

"I can't go back without it," she pleaded. "My uncle… It's one thing when he withholds medicine from me. But now he's threatening my best friend. And my *husband*."

"Your husband." Dorian rolled his shoulders and stuffed his hands into his trouser pockets. "But is he really? I mean, you only married him in two of the timelines."

Isla pressed her lips together as her stare turned to stone. "That's only because the other four timelines were foiled before the wedding took place."

"And you would have gone through with it?" Dorian prodded. "Said 'till death do us part' in all six?" When she refused to answer, he added, "Even the fourth timeline? The one I'm sure you're treated to, as well as I, every time the clock strikes three and nine?"

"Well…I guess we'll never know." Isla yanked the vest on over her frilly blouse and fumbled with the laces. "But I still need that journal."

"I don't know what to tell you," Dorian said. It wasn't a complete lie. Sure, he knew exactly where the journal was. But he'd also sworn to protect it with his life. It had been Ezra's last request before he vanished into thin air.

Just like Elizabeth.

Though Dorian still had no idea how or why. Even with the journal, he feared it was a mystery he may never unravel.

Isla stood and fastened the ratty shawl over her shoulders. Then she snatched her hat off Dorian's head, dusting it against her skirt before donning it again.

"Don't be foolish." She gave him a sad smile. "If I don't bring that journal back, the next person my uncle sends to fetch it won't be so nice."

"Nice?" He barked out a clipped laugh. "Is that what you call this?"

"Would you prefer I be unkind?"

"Oh, I'd prefer a lot of things," he said, letting his gaze sweep over her, up and down until her cheeks turned red. "But I think I've had enough of your *kindness* for one day."

Isla's mouth gaped open, but Dorian only allowed himself a split second to enjoy her furious surprise. Then he turned on his heel and stalked back through the loft and down the stairs. He was out the front door and halfway to the tavern the next block over before she caught up with him.

"How *dare* you," she hissed. "I know you have it. Just

give it to me, and I'll leave you alone."

"I don't have it," he said, holding out his arms. "Would you like to search me?"

She groaned and skipped a step to keep up. "Where is it, then? At the store? Shouldn't you be heading back that way soon? The sign said eleven."

"You were at the store?" Dorian stopped and stared at her. "What were you doing there?"

"I was…looking for you," she admitted clumsily. "Why's the place locked up, anyway? Where's Pearl?"

"She left me—she left," he corrected himself, remembering she had never really been his. For that matter, neither had Isla. "You should, too. Go back to your *husband*," he added, hating the pitying look Isla gave him. The sharpness of his tone wiped it away, bringing back her scowl.

"Not without the journal."

"Suit yourself." Dorian shrugged and resumed his stroll toward the tavern tucked in amongst the other businesses.

This slice of the city was his favorite, with its checkered window frames and winding cobblestone paths. The mismatched brick buildings followed no rhyme or rule, their angles staggering roughly along narrow alleys, with an occasional and unexpected curved wall.

Isla followed close behind, but Dorian supposed the Greasy Gear would end her pursuit soon enough. It wasn't the sort of place Boston's Best would be caught dead in—and definitely not a fancy, uptown lady like Isla.

The bar had been called something else before the Break. But with owners either dying or falling ill or being cut off from their businesses by the fence around the clocked zone, some changes had to be made. Most of all, any establishment with a name that referenced ringing or tolling or bells in general went the way of the dodo. And, naturally, anything that mentioned gears or oil appealed to the more mechanically inclined citizens of Late Boston.

"You're going in there?" Isla balked as he neared the Greasy Gear.

"Yes, ma'am."

"No," she gasped. "It's not even lunchtime."

He gave her a tight grin. "Well, when you spot the ale police, be sure to tell 'em where they can find me." He pushed through the front door and let it close in her face.

Not in a million years would he have expected Isla to follow him. Not after that first time.

Of course, he hadn't expected her to then, either.

And yet, she had.

And again, she did.

Chapter Ten

September 13ᵗʰ, 1916 – 9:42 a.m.

The corset under Isla's wedding dress was too tight. Or maybe it was too warm.

She couldn't breathe. She couldn't think. Her head swam with too many thoughts and not enough oxygen.

What was she doing? She couldn't get married.

Not now. Not today.

Not to him.

Leopold Le Guin deserved better than a halfhearted bride to send him off to his likely death across the Atlantic. Isla was not up to the task. She was no more eager to be a widow than she was to be a wife. Everything was happening too soon.

She paced the small tent that had been set up in the clearing beside the Parkman Bandstand and gulped down breaths as deep as her dress would allow. Four massive bouquets of white roses and lilacs waited on a nearby table. The smell of them was suddenly too much. Sickeningly sweet.

Isla shoved through the slit in the canvas at the back of the tent and bent over the grass, dry heaving as her pulse throbbed in her throat. She heard someone gasp and prayed it wasn't anyone important—important to her uncle, anyway. She'd never hear the end of it.

A cool, gloved hand pressed against the back of her neck, and another cupped her forehead.

"It must be something I had for breakfast," she blurted before gagging again.

"Sure," Mabel agreed, her fingers migrating to Isla's flushed cheeks. "Those two bites of toast you had looked ominous."

"I think I'm going to faint," Isla said, her heaves ebbing back to laborious breathing. "I need to sit down. Or call off the wedding," she added under her breath and gave her friend a pleading look.

"One crisis at a time," Mabel cooed, coaxing her back inside the tent and to a small settee where she'd been instructed to wait for her next cue. It was a habit Isla had grown tired of—waiting for someone to tell her what came next. Dictating how her life should be lived.

When she'd accepted the captain's proposal, she had thought she was finally making a choice for herself. But then her uncle had stuck his fingers in yet another pie, taking over her future husband's military career and orchestrating a hasty wedding.

It's too soon, Isla thought again. Even the captain's mother had had the nerve to inquire if Isla was expecting. If the woman caught her retching up her breakfast in the Common, there'd be no convincing her otherwise.

"Here we go." Mabel poured a glass of water from a pitcher and brought it to Isla. "Little sips," she instructed. "Slowly does it."

Isla obeyed, pausing to breathe in between each swallow. She needed to calm down. Her other two bridesmaids, the captain's sisters Charlotte and Francine, would be there any second.

Mabel sat on the settee beside Isla and cocked her head so her enormous picture hat wouldn't slap her friend in the face. Half a dozen roses trimmed with lace and ribbon decorated the brim of the headpiece. More lace and ribbon were gathered around her neck and at the elbows, wrists, and waist of her dress.

"You look like my wedding cake," Isla said, chuckling. "The boys are going to eat you up."

"And you look like a fairy princess." Mabel fingered one of the blooms on the flower crown over Isla's head. Her veil hung from the back of it, a lacy affair that was nearly as long as her gown.

"Feeling better?" Mabel asked, linking their gloved fingers together.

"I don't think I can do this." Isla swallowed. "It just

doesn't feel right."

The canvas flaps parted, and her father was suddenly in the tent with them, dressed in a gray morning suit and a matching silk top hat.

"I meant to be here sooner," he began. But before he could finish, Isla was in his arms, squeezing him until she felt a vertebra pop in his back. "Goodness," he said with a stiff laugh. "You've grown up. And I've missed it. I've missed you."

"I've missed you, too." Isla beamed and wiped her gloved fingers under her eyes, drying the tears from her lashes. "Oh, Father. I'm getting married."

"So I see." He took a step back to have a better look at her. "And what a lovely bride you are. I hope this airship captain you're marrying knows how lucky he is."

"Oh! You haven't met him yet." Isla grimaced, displeased that reality had crept in so quickly, spoiling their tender reunion. "Will you walk with me anyway? And give your blessing at the altar?"

"Of course." He looked wounded that she had thought he might refuse. But what was she to assume after five years and no word? "I've a special gift for you, too," he said, drawing her thoughts away from unpleasant things. "Though it won't arrive until noon. I hope that's not too late?"

"Not at all." She smiled again, and he opened his hands for hers. They felt smaller than she remembered but just as warm and strong—and safe.

Charlotte and Francine arrived next. Introductions were made, and then the string quartet prompted them to gather up their flowers and head for the altar. Mabel gave Isla a good-luck kiss before leaving her alone in the tent with her father to await the final cue.

The nerves that had been churning Isla's meager breakfast finally yielded, and she found herself thinking that maybe this wasn't so bad. She could face the growing crowd in the Common. Then she could climb the bandstand steps and repeat her wedding vows and promise forever to a man she hardly knew, whom she might never see again after their honeymoon.

All for the sake of not spoiling this special day.

Even if it was meant to be *her* special day.

And with her arm tucked under her father's, it was very nearly perfect. Everything seemed possible again. Everything felt right again. Of course, she would have followed him to the gates of hell if he'd have let her.

Instead, she picked up her bouquet of roses and lilacs and followed him into the park, letting him lead her into the next chapter of her life.

Chapter Eleven

Isla was relentless.

Dorian was impressed, but more than that, he was annoyed.

He dug a quarter out of his pocket and slid it across the counter to Poe, the barkeep who ran the place. The man was mostly bald and half a foot shorter than his wife, Annie, who pitched in whenever the joint got busy. He had to stand on a crate to reach the top shelf behind the bar. But what he lacked in height, he made up for in girth.

Dorian had once watched him carry two casks up from the cellar by himself. At the same time. One over each shoulder. It was enough to make any meathead think twice about crossing him.

"The usual," Dorian requested as Poe picked up the coin.

"And for your lady friend?" he asked.

"Sure." Isla elbowed Dorian in the ribs as she joined him at the counter. "Let's have the usual."

He closed his eyes and groaned. "You shouldn't be here. I'm warning you. This is a rough crowd."

Poe snorted out a sound that crossed somewhere between offended and amused. But he fetched two glass mugs and set to work filling them.

Isla sniffed, unimpressed by the handful of patrons scattered throughout the room. She made a softer, more delighted sound as Pendulum, the tavern cat, hopped onto the bar.

"Look at you," Isla cooed, stroking the little beast's tabby coat and scratching her beneath the chin. One hind leg was enclosed in a bronze sleeve with flexible, cogged joints. The ungrateful mouser growled upon seeing Dorian as if he hadn't risked getting his eyes clawed out to keep her on all fours.

"Penny likes you," Poe said, sliding the mugs of ale across the counter.

"Was she hurt in the Break?" Isla asked, noticing the clockwork cast.

"Just before. Some dandy in a motorcar ran over her back leg," Poe explained. "But Mr. Verne took good care of our little puss."

"Then I's took care of *his* puss." A thick arm wrapped around Dorian's neck and lifted him up onto his toes. He flinched, anticipating the meaty knuckles that scuffed his jaw, teetering between playful and painful.

"That you did," Dorian agreed stiffly, patting the man's arm in surrender.

"Who's your gal, Doris?" Connor Kipling asked, dropping Dorian back onto his feet as his attention migrated to Isla. Of all Poe's regulars at the Greasy Gear, Kipling was the most obnoxious. The man had a permanent sneer, and a jaw so sharp it was a wonder he didn't slice the sleeve off his jacket anytime he wiped the foam from the cleft in his chin.

Kipling chugged what was left of his ale in a single go, his eyes never leaving Isla. Then he set his mug down hard on the bartop. The noise drew a hiss from Pendulum. The cat's fur stood on end, and she bolted from the counter, taking shelter under a table in the corner.

"This is Isla Huxley—" Dorian began.

"Le Guin," she corrected, shooting him a sideways glare.

"Isla Le Guin," he relented. "She's an old friend of mine." He hoped an introduction would stave off whatever venomous words Isla looked ready to hurl at Kipling. "And she's married," he added, in case it wasn't clear from the last name mishap. It wasn't something he would have openly admitted or emphasized if he'd thought there was a better way to keep the drunken behemoth in line.

"Don't see your kind in here often," Kipling said, waving his hand at Poe for a refill.

"I should hope not." Isla turned her nose up.

"Ain't never met a *married* working girl afore."

"Working girl!" Her fists balled, and Dorian reacted on instinct. He took hold of Isla's waist and pulled her away from the bar, trying to decide how to navigate the situation without earning himself a shiner—from her or Kipling.

"It's all right, princess." Kipling chuckled, clearly proud of himself for having crawled under her skin so swiftly and effectively. "I's had to get me a new job after the Break, too."

"I've got a break for you!" Isla stamped a heel on Dorian's foot, struggling to get loose, but he held tight. The second she got her hands on Kipling, the dominos would begin to fall. And Dorian knew exactly where they'd land. The same place they always did. Right on his head.

The door swung open, and Frank and Philip, two more regulars who ran a printing shop up the street, entered the tavern as they often did, in the middle of an argument. Something about paper quality or quantity. Dorian wasn't sure, his attention too torn between Kipling and Isla.

"Well, hello," Frank crooned. "What have we here?"

"Is there a Mrs. Verne we haven't had the pleasure of meeting?" Philip guessed aloud, tossing a handful of dimes on the bartop.

Dorian could see why he might assume so, with how his arms were wrapped around Isla's middle. And despite the ache in his toes, he rather enjoyed the way her back felt pressed against his chest. Even with the ostrich feather of her hat tickling his nose again.

"No," he answered before Isla could tell Phillip off for the insinuation. "Just a friend."

"Hardly." She made a face at him, but it lacked the contempt she redirected at Kipling, who was sloshing down another ale. Poe brought him a third as he delivered Frank's and Philip's.

"Pity." Frank sighed and leaned against the bar, taking his mug in hand. "We could use some good news about now."

"Trouble with the press?" Poe asked. He dipped his chin in a grateful nod at Phillip for the penny tip the man flipped to him.

"Always." Phillip sucked the foam from the top of his glass. When he made it to the dark nectar, he took a long drink and moaned his contentment. "The ol' clock-knockers wised up," he continued. "They switched to a thicker paper—a kind we don't have access to and have no way of replicating."

Frank hung his head. "And just when we'd figured out the new ink colors."

"You're forging ration booklets?" Isla said, her eyebrows drawing together.

Phillip stared at her before turning to Dorian. "Who's this now?"

"Only a friend, and we were on our way out," Dorian answered, deciding Isla could annoy him just as easily back at the store. It was safer. And besides that, the whiskey was cheaper there.

Frank squinted at Isla. "I've seen you somewhere."

"Doubtful," Dorian said, releasing Isla's waist and taking her by the elbow to better steer her toward the exit. "She's not from around here."

Isla snorted and yanked her arm free. "Not anymore."

"No, I've definitely seen your face. The paper!" He snapped his fingers. "That's it. There was a big engagement announcement—oh. Oh, dear…" Frank blanched, and Dorian could practically read the details of the article through the man's fearful eyes.

"Yes, well, we best be going," he said, taking Isla by the arm again.

"What's the hurry, Doris?" Kipling took a sloppy pull from his mug and smacked his lips. "Seems we got a celebrity on our hands. Why not tell us all about her?"

Isla rolled her eyes. "Do you harass all the ladies this way?"

"If you wanted to be treated like a lady, you've come to the wrong place," Kipling slurred. "Or the wrong time. But haven't we all?" He cackled and slapped his elbow down on the bar, sliding it through spilled beer and peanut shells. "Know what I was afore the Break, princess?"

"A poet?" Isla snapped.

"No, though I been known to sing a sailor's song or two," Kipling said, flexing his right hand. Each knuckle was ringed with a bronze fitting connected to an intricate assembly of braces and hinges. They squeaked and clinked as his fingers moved. "I had me a sweet little cargo ship that'd gone all the way around the world— probably more times than you've turned tricks."

"You pig!" Isla snarled.

Dorian's grip on her arm tightened, but Isla's attention latched on to their forgotten mugs. Before he could stop her, Kipling was drenched in ale. Foam dripped down his nose and cheeks, saturating the front of his jacket and the shirt beneath. His sneer sharpened, and an eager twinkle lit his eyes.

"Stand back," Dorian hissed, pushing Isla behind him and toward the door. He never liked what came next, but there was no need for her to be part of it. Kipling was already rolling up his jacket sleeve when Dorian turned around.

"I'll use me good hand so's I don't muck up your pretty face," he said, curling his fist back.

Dorian yanked his goggles off and stuffed them into his pocket. If he didn't fight back, Kipling was generally satisfied with a single punch. He angled his chin to one side and winced in anticipation. But before he could take his lump and go, Phillip scooped up a chair from a nearby table and whacked it across Kipling's back, laying him out flat.

A leg wobbled loose from the seat, and Poe let out a dejected sigh as it clattered to the floor. Phillip picked it up and attempted to fit it back in its hole, but it was no use. The thing had reached its brawl quota. *Its Kipling quota, more like*, thought Dorian as he inched toward the door.

"Oh, bother," Philip tutted. He shot Poe an apologetic smile, but quickly discarded both chair and leg as Kipling rose from the floor.

"Who done that?" he demanded, spinning in a

clumsy circle. "I'll clobber every last one of yous. Fess up, now, you cowards."

"Ah, hell," Frank sighed. "Why not?" He finished off his ale, then gripped the handle of the mug tightly as he spun around and cracked Kipling upside the head with it. Glass shattered, and blood squirted from Kipling's lower lip.

Poe loosed an annoyed huff, contrasting with Isla's gasp of horror.

Dorian was mortified. He wanted to drag her out of there while everyone was distracted. Of course, he'd never be able to show his face at the Greasy Gear again. Not without Kipling rearranging it for him. Fleeing a brawl was the ultimate sin. Though no more sinful than putting Isla in harm's way. And, Dorian decided, keeping all his teeth was a decent silver lining.

He turned to grab Isla, only to find her creeping forward with her empty mug clutched in both hands, eyes gleaming with malice.

Frank's blow hadn't knocked Kipling off his feet, though it had sent him reeling about the room until his eyes refocused—well, as much as they could while floating in ale. He placed a hand on either side of his face as he wobbled about, bronze-plated fingers digging into his right cheek. But as Isla lunged forward, his gaze narrowed.

"Isla, wait!" Dorian stepped between them, holding his arms out to warn her off. He took a hard fist to the ear for his efforts. Then Kipling was on his back, tackling him to the floor. The scuffle didn't last long. Thanks to Isla's well-aimed mug that caught Kipling across the temple.

Dorian groaned and pulled himself up off the floor. He opened his mouth wide and shook his head, trying to stop the ringing in his ear. The cartilage ached something awful.

"I don't need you to defend my honor," Isla said, though worry seeped through her words. She touched his arm until he looked up at her.

"I'm fine," he answered automatically. "I mean, you're welcome. Or well done."

He couldn't decide which answer annoyed her most. Maybe all of them. But she didn't have time to tell him about it. Kipling was lurching to his feet again.

More blood trickled from a new cut across his forehead, but something close to reverence tinged the man's swimming eyes when he next set his sights on Isla. Dorian wasn't sure if that was a good thing or a bad thing. He didn't want it to be a thing at all. He would have preferred to be the only one who looked at Isla that way.

And to prove the point, he put himself in Kipling's path once again.

The tension in the room swelled, gazes darting this way and that as everyone tried to guess who would strike next and who would be the recipient. There was an air of danger, but also one of camaraderie. Except for maybe Poe, who silently seethed at the damage to his tavern.

"You knuckleheads done yet?" he barked. "The clock's about to have its turn."

Dorian reflexively touched his forehead where his goggles should have been. He swore and reached for his pocket, but it was too late.

The first strike of the eleven o'clock bell echoed out over the city. The building shuddered, and the glassware rattled on the tavern shelves.

"Oh, bother," Phillip groaned and crawled under a table in the corner—the same table Pendulum happened to be under. She mewled pitifully at him.

Frank leaned against the far end of the bar and waved for Poe to fetch him another pint, ignoring the quake altogether, while Kipling wobbled no more and no less than he always did after drowning his senses in ale. And he was no bloodier than usual either, Dorian noted. Though one of his bronze fingers did appear to be bent at a wrong angle.

"Dorian," Isla whispered, her voice quivering as she grasped the bartop. Cold terror stretched the black of her eyes until only a thin ring of amber remained.

It suddenly occurred to Dorian that the Post Boston Infirmary was a good deal farther away from the clock tower than Poe's tavern. Not that it mattered. He was sure Isla had suffered plenty there, too. But witnessing it was so much worse than he could have ever imagined. He would have given anything to keep her from enduring another bell.

No promise was worth that.

No dream meant more than keeping her from harm.

He eased closer to Isla, placing one hand on the counter and wrapping his other around her waist. She closed her eyes and tucked her head into the crook of his neck.

"I've got you," he rasped. "Everything's going to be okay."

Chapter Twelve

December 13th, 1916 – 11:16 a.m.

Isla did not want to puke her guts up in front of Dorian and his *friends*.

That's what they were, she realized, watching him stitch up Connor Kipling's face and readjust his metallic fingers. The bells had had a sobering effect on the man, but he distracted himself from Dorian's doctoring by telling Isla all about his previous life as an opium smuggler and his many adventures in the Orient and the Caribbean.

The mention of poppies made her stomach roil greedily. She was sick with need and panic after experiencing the full weight of the bells. But Dorian had given her a peculiar look when she'd asked Kipling if he was a consumer as well as a courier, so she refrained from any additional prying.

"Smashed me hand here between the wharf and me boat when I abandoned ship," he explained, holding up his bronze fingers for closer inspection.

"I'll have to come back with my kit later and tighten things up, but that should do for now," Dorian said, wiping his hands on a bar rag Poe had loaned him.

"Fair enough, Doris," Kipling replied before going back to his sad tale. "They picked her clean of me payload, killed me crew, and then hauled her off to a dock guarded by the clock-knockers."

Isla had wondered how Orwell had come into so much morphine and laudanum. Now she knew. She supposed that was why his laboratories were operational even after the Break, though she still had questions. The more troubling ones were for her uncle, and she doubted she'd ever have the nerve to pose them. But one did seem harmless enough for the rowdy crowd at the Greasy Gear.

"Clock-knockers?" she inquired.

"Another name for the timekeepers," Dorian said. "Orwell's men, who guard the infirmary, the waterfront, and the quarantine fence from the inside."

"They knock around us folk cursed by the clock, you see?" Frank added, still nursing the ale he'd ordered amid the bells.

"Ah." Isla nodded, accepting the nickname without objection. It was fitting.

The few officers who had been trapped in Late Boston after the Break and had pledged themselves to her uncle's cause were a different breed than the city had known before. They were desperate and vicious—they had to be. Orwell kept them on a tight leash. If they didn't do what they were told, their families would be worse off than the citizens unwelcome at the infirmary, without a home or ration to their name. Unless, of course, they came by one of the counterfeit books from Frank and Phillip's print shop.

"If you tell anyone at the infirmary, we're good as dead," Frank reminded Isla as she and Dorian left the tavern. She locked her lips with an invisible key and waved goodbye, even offering Kipling a small smile as he wiggled his squeaky fingers at her.

"Strange lot you're running with these days," she said, letting Dorian take her by the hand. A grin pinched one corner of his mouth when she didn't protest.

They followed Union Street to Adam's Square and turned down Washington, heading back through Downtown Crossing on their way to the Clockwork Apothecary.

Isla received fewer cross stares in her mother's ratty shawl, but she did notice the kinder glances aimed at Dorian. And when she looked closer, she realized many of the people sported some mechanical prosthetic or another. Copper collars hidden beneath scarves, brass braces poking out of boots and coat sleeves.

"Where did all the metal come from?" Isla asked as

they neared the store.

"The other bells." Dorian's brows hitched as if it were obvious. "From the Old North Church, Faneuil Hall, King's Chapel. They were all taken to a bronzesmith in North End, then melted down and refashioned into parts more useful to the victims of Late Boston."

"Are you the only one tending to them?" she asked next.

"Pearl was, too." With his free hand, Dorian fetched a key from his satchel. "And, sometimes, Dr. Doyle. But he's not in the best health. And then Pearl decided to go to the infirmary."

Isla gasped. "Whatever for?"

"She's too kind. Too good," he replied, shaking his head. "Thanks to Kipling, we all know how your uncle treats the Break's effects on Boston's Best." Dorian gave Isla a telling glance that she was too ashamed to hold. "I assume that's the *medicine* he's denying you?"

"Poppy tea and laudanum. For me, anyway. Morphine for Mabel and the captain."

"But the opiates won't last forever." Dorian squeezed her hand and stared at the lock on the front door as if trying to determine if he could manage it without releasing her. Isla made the decision for him and extracted her fingers from his grasp. She'd indulged a child's wish for long enough—hers and his.

"So, Pearl intends to share your clockwork remedies at the infirmary," she said as Dorian set to work unlocking the store. "That's why she left?"

"In part. But mostly, I think, to get away from me," he added with a bitter smile.

"Mr. Verne!" A young boy of maybe twelve pedaled a bicycle up the street. A dozen paper sacks were crowded in a basket between the handlebars, and as he rolled to a stop, he handed one off to Dorian. "Thanks again for taking care of my pop this morning. He was in bad shape."

"Anytime, Peter." Dorian ruffled the kid's hair before he peddled away. "Just wish I had a cog that could survive the man's tobacco habit," he said under his breath, handing the sack off to Isla.

"I'm starving," she confessed. The smell of fresh bread and hot cheese wafted up from the package. She'd eaten breakfast only a few hours ago, and it had been all she could do to choke down a handful of strawberries and a slice of buttered bread. All the panicking and walking and fighting had worked up an appetite.

"Come on." Dorian pushed the front door open and waved her inside. "I have coffee and soup upstairs. I'll fix us lunch before you resume badgering me about your father's journal."

"You have coffee?" Isla grinned and hurried after him, deciding she could postpone her quest a bit longer. Who could turn down a good kaffeeklatsch in times such as these?

"You may be stuck here through the noon bells," Dorian warned as they cut through the dark store and headed up the stairwell. "But I may have something to ease the distress."

"Poppy tea?"

"No." He laughed. "Your uncle has the market on that, I'm afraid."

"A clockwork remedy, then?"

"Not quite. You'll see."

Sunlight streamed through a wide window at the front of the apartment. Isla noted a stack of books on the sill, many of their spines worn and familiar. She wondered if her father had given them to Dorian or if he'd collected them from the workshop after the Break. Bits of paper poked from their text blocks, bookmarking dozens of pages.

Isla set the pastry sack on a table and glanced around the small living space while Dorian fiddled with a percolator in the kitchen, which was really no more than a few cupboards and a sink, wedged beside a large, cast-iron stove that consumed one whole corner.

The dining table was larger than Isla would have expected for Dorian's family, which had never consisted of more than three as far as she was aware. But, from the stained and scarred surface, she imagined the Vernes had used it for more than just sharing meals.

It reminded her of the table in the loft above her father's workshop, a beast of old oak that dwarfed an already tiny space. A space that had been full of love and laughter and dreams. Nothing like the cold dining room at her uncle's manor, used explicitly for dinner parties.

Dorian's home was larger than the loft Isla had grown up in. A writing desk and a pair of dusty wingback chairs filled the other side of the room. The rest of the apartment was tucked away down a narrow hall that curled into the belly of the building. That was where Dorian's bedroom was.

Isla's breath hitched as her mind grasped at a vision. It was like trying to remember forgotten fragments of a dream. Or *déjà vu*, as Madam Pittard would have called it.

She'd read about the timeline with Dorian in her journal, in the notes she'd gathered at the onset of each shift in time. But it was like reading about someone else's life. Once the hours passed, the finer details slipped from her mind, leaving only the raw data behind.

It was the same way with the captain. At the eleven o'clock bell, she'd lost another hour of the morning before her wedding. She didn't remember Mabel stroking her hair or opening the bedroom curtains. And the ceremony at the Common was a gaping black hole in her mind.

It would all come back at noon, she reminded herself. That much she understood from her notes. And then she would be sick with shame for the way she'd behaved today. Brawling in a tavern and parading through the ravaged city, hand-in-hand with her childhood sweetheart.

She frowned at Dorian, still busy at the stove in the kitchen, and then wandered over to his disheveled reading nook near the window, hoping to distract herself until the coffee was ready. Dorian's library would have seemed irrelevant to anyone outside of Late Boston, with volumes on anatomy and medical journals scattered amongst machine works magazines and parts catalogs.

"Is this where you keep my father's journal?" she asked, picking up a manual on clock maintenance.

"Uh…no." Dorian snorted out a humorless laugh as he set the table with bowls and coffee cups. "You really can't wait to get back there, can you?"

Isla's cheeks burned at the accusation. That hadn't

been the reason for her question, though she couldn't deny that she was looking forward to the Milk of Paradise her uncle had promised upon her returned with the journal. Opium had been her only means of getting through the bells, and now it was her master. Not that she owed Dorian any explanation or apology for it.

Rather than argue those points with him, she held up her father's battered copy of Voight's *Lehrbuch der Kristallphysik.*

"When did you take up German?" she asked, a snide note in her voice. "Or crystal physics, for that matter?"

Dorian sighed and turned back to the stove, stirring the soup once more before turning the burner down. "Your father left plenty of notes in the margins."

The next book on the stack was *Cristallographie* by Jean-Baptiste Romé. Isla pushed it to one side, finding more volumes on piezoelectricity and thermodynamics and alternating currents. Her heart fluttered like a bird anticipating being pounced on by a cat.

"What is the meaning of all this, Dorian?"

"Come have some coffee," he said, reaching for the book clutched in her hands.

"No!" She wrenched it away from him and glanced at the stairs. The book she held wasn't her father's journal, but if it had been, she would have made a run for it.

Not because her guts had begun to churn anew with anxiety and craving. But because finding these books in Dorian's collection could only mean one thing. He was up to absolutely no good.

"Okay." He held up one hand in surrender and slipped his other into his pocket, retrieving the goggles he'd worn when she first encountered him. "Look, I used some of the crystal from the workshop to make these."

He held them out to her, waving his free hand in a silent request to trade for the book. Isla complied, snatching the goggles before retreating to the corner to inspect them.

"Why would you do that?" she demanded. "What are they for?"

"They're *my* remedy for the bells. In retrospect, I probably shouldn't have wasted the crystal it took to make them. But they do make the time shifts more bearable."

"How could this possibly help anything?"

"I know what I'm doing." Dorian replaced the book on the windowsill with the others and motioned for her to follow him back downstairs. "Come on. I'll show you."

Isla didn't take his hand this time. She clutched the

purple goggles, running her thumbs nervously over the shallow facets of their lenses. But she followed Dorian.

It was a short journey to the storeroom on the main floor. Dorian fetched another key and an oil lamp before leading her inside. A long table rested against one wall, crowded with familiar machinery and tools that Isla recognized from her father's workshop. And then she saw it.

"What have you done?" she whispered. The amethyst glow of the crystals burned her eyes, now wet with unshed tears.

"It's not finished," he admitted hollowly. "I can't find any more oraclyst."

"Small mercy."

Dorian's gaze snapped back to her, his eyes brimming with wounded pride. "It's your father's design."

"My father was a careless monster who destroyed this city, Dorian."

"It wasn't his fault—"

"It's *all* his fault!" Isla dragged a hand over her face. "We don't need another machine. We need to figure out how to fix the one in the tower. Or shut it down."

"It can't be shut down," Dorian insisted. He grabbed an open book off a nearby stool and held it up for her to see, pointing at a drawing of a gear train over a platform.

"Look. The battery is pulled backward through time, like our memories. It recharges itself."

Isla sniffled and blinked back her tears, straining to read her father's handwriting. She held her breath as she touched the swirling ink on the page. It was dangerous, delicate work. Both her father's and her own as she gently extracted the book from Dorian's hands.

"This doesn't look the same as what you're building," Isla said, her gaze flicking up at the crystal ring on the back wall.

"But it is!" Dorian took the invitation for what it was and turned to admire his work. He crossed the small room and pointed out the copper wires around the frame. "Only my clock will be less complicated, run by a mainspring instead of weights."

Isla didn't wait to hear what he said next.

She clutched the journal to her chest and stepped out into the hall, slamming the door closed behind her. The key was still inserted in the lock. She gave it a twist just as the handle rattled and Dorian's fist connected with the other side of the door.

"Isla! What are you doing?"

"What I have to," she said, backing away from his mounting anger, muffled as it was, and squeezed the book tighter to her chest.

"You can't give it to Orwell," he shouted. "He'll ruin everything."

"You already have," Isla whispered, more to herself than to Dorian.

She cut through the store and stumbled out onto the street before taking off at a sprint toward the Common. The park was empty, but her relief staled when she realized it was only because she'd lost track of time. It was nearly noon.

No, Isla thought as the first bell rolled like thunder overhead, *it* is *noon.*

She made it to Brewer Fountain before the fourth toll sent her to her knees. The stoic Greek effigies inspired by watery myths ignored her from their perch above the fountain's basin. Neptune and Amphitrite, Acis and Galatea. They didn't care that it felt as if the clock's hammer was striking Isla's brain instead of the cursed bell.

The memories of her wedding day unfurled in her mind like one of her uncle's Persian rugs, just before the maids beat the dust and dirt from it. Sensory details crawled under her skin, forcing her to relive those lost hours in the slivers of time that stretched between the bell tolls.

That's when she remembered Dorian's goggles, still

clenched in her fist.

She threw her hat aside and tried to put the goggles on with one hand, not wanting to let go of the journal. But when the next bell doubled her over, she caved, releasing everything to clutch her head in her hands.

The bronze figures seated around the fountain looked on indifferently, unaffected by the bells or the stiff winds of winter. Isla wanted to trade places with Neptune. She didn't want to be made of flesh and blood anymore.

As if in answer to her prayer, the Greek god called out to her. "You're all right now, poppet."

Isla blinked up at him, watching as his face morphed from cool bronze to ruddy flesh. She pried her hands away from her head and looked down at her fingers, wondering if they'd begun to change, too.

Had she fallen upon some strange spiritual alchemy?

Was she to be baptized in the fountain?

Or simply drowned by the man in the paperboy cap who suddenly had ahold of her arm?

It didn't matter. Anything had to be better than this, Isla decided as the next bell cracked her mind open like an egg, and her world went black.

Chapter Thirteen

September 13th, 1916 – 10:52 a.m.

It was done.

Isla was married.

She was Mrs. Leopold Le Guin. Wife of a brave airship captain who was kind and handsome and rich and everything any girl could ever want. He would probably win the war single-handedly, with nothing more than a charming smile and a handshake, like he'd given Dorian when Isla had introduced them at the reception.

Dorian Verne, a local clocksmith, her childhood friend.

Well, that was him. Nothing more, nothing less. And nothing he thought would convince Isla to give up a posh life with a *real* captain, respected and admired by all of Boston.

No. It was much too late now. Besides, Dorian had heard her loud and clear.

Till death do us part.

She'd professed her vows before all these fancy people—people who kept giving Dorian and Pearl spiteful glances from the corners of their eyes. They didn't belong here. Though tidy and appropriate for such an occasion, their clothes were not the latest fashions found at the boutiques on Charles Street. Though the suit Ezra had arrived in looked as though it might have been plucked right out of a display window.

Dorian had been more than a little surprised that Isla's father arrived on time, and looking as gussied-up as her uncle, at that. Isla was every bit as delighted as he'd thought she'd be. And her uncle was spitting mad. Half the reason Dorian wanted to stick around for the remainder of the reception was to enjoy the man's discomfort. He'd been the source of plenty for Dorian, and turnabout was fair play. Dorian couldn't even feel guilty for the satisfaction it brought him.

The other half of his reason for staying had to do with Pearl. Eight years, and he'd only ever taken her to ball games and a funeral. She was so tickled to be at a ritzy wedding in the Common. Dorian had never seen her smile so brightly.

The pink dress Dr. Doyle had given Pearl as a birthday gift was pretty, even if it was meant for a spring tea party, with its short lace sleeves and satin belt. Dorian didn't care. She was a vision regardless. Her pale blond locks were swept up in a Gibson Girl bun, and she'd added a purple ribbon to her straw boater hat—fully committing to the spring faux pas.

It reminded Dorian of the necklace burning a hole in his pocket.

The old woman who'd stopped him on the street that morning lingered in his mind. She'd been hysterical, certainly. But familiar, too. And, most troubling of all, she'd known his name.

There's still time, Dorian. She needs you.

The piece of jewelry had spooked Ezra, as well. And after the way the new machine in the clock tower reacted, it was clear that the pendant was made of oraclyst.

Of course, when nothing more happened beyond the shorting out of one of the machine's crystal portals, Ezra had shoved the necklace back into Dorian's hand and sent him off to get ready for Isla's wedding.

Dorian retrieved the pendant and held it up in the sunlight. It was rare and beautiful. It belonged around a rare and beautiful girl's neck. Not in his pocket.

Just then, Pearl crossed the lawn, returning from dancing a playful waltz with Dr. Doyle. They'd been practicing all week. She stopped suddenly, noticing the necklace in Dorian's hand. Careful curiosity lit her eyes, and a small smile quivered across her lips.

A wedding gift? she signed.

Dorian shook his head, marveling at his ignorance. The rarest beauty of all was right in front of him. But did she need him? Could Pearl be the one the woman on the street had meant? Or had knowing his name been a co-incidence? Maybe she was just a looney old crone, roaming the streets with found treasures, puzzling any-one naïve enough to indulge her.

He laughed at himself and unclasped the necklace, holding it up to Pearl until she understood he meant to put it on her. Her smile quivered again, dropping away suddenly only to reappear brighter than the sun. She turned around, giving him better access to her neck.

Dorian draped the pendant across her throat and fas-tened the cord above the lace collar of her dress. Her cheeks flushed as she faced him again.

Thank you, she signed, touching her gloved fingertips to her chin.

It didn't matter who or what the woman on the street was talking about, Dorian decided. He smiled and nod-ded at the small area near the bandstand where guests were dancing. Even though Pearl certainly knew he couldn't tell the difference between a waltz or a foxtrot, she eagerly slipped her hand into his.

Dorian felt her breath hitch beneath his fingers as he touched her waist. Had he always had this effect on Pearl? What an oblivious fool he'd been, his head lost in the clouds with visions of a future that belonged to another man. Those dreams hadn't been meant for him.

But that didn't mean he couldn't make new dreams with Pearl, did it? Or maybe Pearl would share the ones she'd clearly been holding on to for the both of them.

Dorian dipped his chin down close to her ear and breathed in the floral warmth of her skin. "You're the loveliest girl here," he whispered, pressing a kiss to her cheek that made her blush even fiercer.

A strange calm fell over the park. For a moment, Dorian thought it was only in his head. A harbinger of the peaceful transition of his affection as he tried to be happy for Isla and, at the same time, devote himself to Pearl.

But when the other guests stopped dancing, he knew something was wrong.

"What is *that*?" A woman pointed off in the distance.

"It's coming from the Custom House Tower," someone else shouted over the growing din.

"The new clock…it's glowing."

"How queer."

Dorian twisted his neck, gazing up at the amethyst haze seeping from the clock's face. It was spreading fast. The earth trembled, and the first toll of the eleven o'clock bell echoed out over Boston. The sound sang through Dorian's bones, ten times more grueling than it had been when standing next to the clock in the tower. It didn't make sense.

Pearl clung to him as he scanned the park, searching for Isla and Ezra. The task became more difficult after the second toll, when screams tore through the Common. Guests tripped and fell over chairs in their attempt to escape, but there was nowhere to go. Nowhere the resounding bells couldn't follow now that the clock had placed its mark upon them.

The third assault of the bell hit Dorian square in the chest. Or maybe that was Isla's scream.

She and Captain Le Guin stood under the bandstand near a folding camera that had been set up to take their wedding photos. Isla grasped her husband's arm, scarcely managing to stay upright as the earth ruptured around the structure's base. The marble columns trembled, cracking with the fourth toll of the bell.

"Isla!" Ezra appeared across the lawn. He steadied himself against a tree, his old knees wobbling as he attempted to get his daughter's attention. "Get out of there!" he shouted.

But everyone was being too loud. Everyone, except Dorian and Pearl. Shock had been to blame at first—for Dorian, anyway. Pearl cried silently against his chest, her eyes squeezed shut and breath rushing in and out against his neck. He held her close, his attention split between Isla, Ezra, and the cracks in the earth quickly spreading across the Common.

The next toll of the bell was the last one Dorian remembered. At least, from this timeline.

The marble columns shattered, and the heavy dome of the bandstand collapsed.

Isla's final scream was smothered by the deafening crush of stone on granite.

Chapter Fourteen

December 13th, 1916 – 1:02 p.m.

Isla's breath hissed as she came to, the taste of death fresh on her tongue.

None of the bells were pleasant, but reliving her death was definitely the most painful. Physically, anyway.

Her skin was gritty with dried sweat, and her chest ached from when all the air had been forced from her lungs. Fortunately, more was immediately pumped in through her oxygen mask.

"Welcome back, kitten." Winifred leaned over her hospital bed and offered a weak smile. "We nearly lost you."

"I wish you would have," Isla grumbled through her mask.

She glanced around her hospital room, wondering if it had always been this small. Had she really lived here for three months? So mortified by her past actions that she'd been willing to stay drugged in this corner of the chessboard until her uncle had needed a new pawn?

Had she always hated herself this much?

"Can you sit up?" Winifred asked, offering Isla her arm.

"Why?" Isla glowered, not only at the idea of moving but at the splitting headache that was so much worse than she remembered. "Where's my tea?"

"Mr. Orwell would like to see you first," Winifred replied with a pitying smile.

"I… I had the journal in my hands."

Winifred nodded grimly. "Yes, and now it's in your uncle's."

"Then why can't he let me be?" she groaned. "I did what he asked."

Winifred sniffed. "When has that ever satisfied your uncle?"

Cold sweat joined the headache, sending a shiver through Isla as she rose from the bed, the covers falling away. Dirt and grass stains marred her white blouse, and the laces of the corset vest she'd borrowed from her mother's trunk had come undone. The fur shawl was nowhere to be found, likely discarded in the park after being mistaken for a dead animal. Isla's heart twinged miserably at the idea, nostalgia forgiving the garment's wretched condition.

"Easy does it," Winifred fussed, delicately removing the mask from Isla's face. "Keep your chin up—I'll see to it that you get what you need," she added in a whisper as if she suspected a nurse could be listening outside the door.

Isla nodded, pausing stiffly as the headache intensified with every little movement. Her stomach growled, and she suddenly remembered the lunch Dorian had been preparing for them—right before her rude departure.

Dorian.

She hoped he was all right. Maybe someone had found him before his coffee had gone cold. His heart was another matter. Isla was sure it had frozen the second she'd turned the key in the storeroom's lock.

She wouldn't tell her uncle about the crystal portal, she decided. It wasn't as if Dorian could do any real harm with it being unfinished, anyway. Though she was still amazed that he'd understood enough of her father's work to figure out how to begin the experiment in the first place. Orwell would undoubtedly send his time-keepers to seize the device and whatever additional research Dorian had done. Then she remembered how Kipling's crew had been taken care of and sucked in a ragged breath at the thought of the same fate befalling Dorian.

"Are you cold?" Winifred asked, squeezing Isla's quivering hand as she helped her out of bed. Before Isla could answer, Winifred slipped out of her lab coat and wrapped it around Isla's shoulders. "This will keep you warm for now," she said, pressing a hand to the middle of Isla's back and directing her toward the door.

Orwell's office was a short walk from the west wing of the infirmary. Too short, Isla decided, wishing she'd had more time to prepare herself before seeing him again. It took something out of her to face her uncle. It was as if he knew how to siphon all the air from a room, all the hope and joy, with only a look. Or a single word.

"Sit," he ordered, not bothering to look up from the journal spread open on his desk.

Winifred nudged her toward one of the leather arm-chairs, but Isla refused. It had taken so much energy just to make it this far, and now her nerves were too twitchy for her to sit still. Her skin itched, and the hunger rolling through her guts teetered on the brink of nausea.

"That's the journal you wanted, isn't it?" she snapped.

Orwell finally looked up at her, surprised annoyance arching his brows. His gaze darted to the empty chair, silently reprimanding her disobedience.

"What more do you want from me?" Isla's voice trembled. She was on the verge of tears. Or screaming. Or dying.

No, she decided. Dying would be too easy. Her uncle

would never allow that.

He sighed and lifted her father's journal, turning it around to show her a technical drawing of a single crystal ring.

"Look familiar?" Orwell said, disgust compounding his meaning.

Isla's heart stammered out a warning, but then Orwell's finger tapped a note in Dorian's handwriting at the bottom corner of the page. Next to it was a small drawing of a pendant necklace. Isla blinked slowly, trying to remember where she'd seen it before.

"This damn journal is useless without the quartz key mentioned here," Orwell spat. "Didn't you take the time to read it before coming back? Didn't you think to ask the boy for whatever other useful information or resources he might possess?"

Isla nearly choked on her next breath. Winifred was right. He would never be satisfied.

"You know he has it, don't you?" Orwell said, dropping the journal back to his desk. "Of course, you'll be going back to fetch it."

"What?" She took a step back, shaking her head.

"Does your husband mean so little to you? And what of poor Mabel?" Orwell tsked, but his disappointment was lacking and glazed with triumph. He'd already won, and he knew it.

"I can't go back," Isla stammered. "Even if Dorian has it, he'll never give it to me now. Not after I stole the journal from him."

"Shall I send my men in to fetch it?"

"No!" Isla thought again of Kipling's crew. "I…I'll do it."

She'd always known her uncle was a dangerous man, but it had been an abstract impression that lurked in the back of her mind. After all, he would never hurt *her*. Not in any obvious way that could tarnish his image among Boston's Best.

"Good girl," Orwell said, snapping the book shut. He flicked his hand toward the office door. "Off you go. Winifred has another coat for you. Try not to *lose* this one."

Isla had enough sense not to ask for medicine before she left. It would do no good, and she couldn't stomach the idea of begging her uncle for something so insignificant with the threats he'd let hang in the air between them, unspoken though crystal clear.

Besides, Winifred had promised to take care of her. As she helped Isla into a black wool coat, she shot a meaningful glance down at one of the garment's front pockets.

"Be careful," she whispered, hugging Isla in the lobby of the west wing. "Even kittens must be weaned."

The wind was colder than Isla remembered, despite the new coat and the comfortable weight of the laudanum bottle knocking against her thigh with every step. Isla was tempted to go find a dark corner of the city and take a poppy nap. She certainly wasn't ready to see Dorian again.

She wondered if he was still locked in the storeroom where she'd left him. Shame stabbed at her conscience as she considered the possibility of quietly sneaking inside his apartment, finding the necklace, and leaving undetected.

It would be no more awful than what she'd already done to him.

Then she could crawl back into her hospital bed, drink a big cup of tea, and sleep until her uncle erased this version of their world. It wouldn't take long. Not with Isla delivering everything he demanded anytime he stuck Mabel or Le Guin's head under the guillotine. And now Dorian's, too.

She passed through the infirmary's front gate, not making eye contact with the officers on guard. Her skin crawled as she wondered if any of them had helped ransack Kipling's ship or murder his crew. But was she any better, fetching these items her uncle demanded when she knew that whatever the outcome of Late Boston, Dorian would not survive it?

The clocksmith had escaped her uncle's wrath too long as it was. As soon as the timeline was righted, he was done for, and the part Isla played in his demise made her feel every bit a killer as the timekeepers. It didn't matter that refusing her uncle would have been a death sentence for Dorian, as well—and likely a much swifter one.

She was only buying him a little time. And breaking both their hearts in the process.

An angry, defeated lump pushed into Isla's throat as she cut across the Common. She didn't want to do this, but she also didn't know what else she *could* do.

Madam Pittard would have called it a paradox. Like one knowing that they knew nothing.

Isla just called it hell.

But she walked through it anyway.

Chapter Fifteen

September 13ᵗʰ, 1916 – 9:53 a.m.

The ceremony would begin any minute. And Ezra still had not arrived.

Dorian couldn't help but feel at least partly responsible. The necklace had been alarming, even for him. Though not quite as disturbing as the woman who had pressed it into his palm and delivered a cryptic message before hobbling off toward the subway.

There's still time, Dorian. She needs you.

Was there still time? Did Isla need him?

He abandoned the back row of wooden folding chairs where he and Pearl had been tucked in between Dr. Doyle and several of Orwell's laboratory managers and strolled deeper into the park, tracing a wide path around the bandstand.

A small tent had been set up for Isla and her bridesmaids. The white canvas was plainer than the candy-striped big tops Isla's governess had taken them to as children, though it was certainly more elegant. Ribbons and flowers dotted the scalloped trim along the top, keeping in theme with the decorations on every tree and table and chair spread across the lawn around the bandstand.

Dorian spied the split entrance of the tent just as a dark-haired woman emerged with an empty water pitcher in her gloved hands. She wore a lacey white gown and an obnoxiously oversized hat strewn with more flowers and ribbon.

She must be a bridesmaid, Dorian decided. He waited for her to disappear around the other side of the tent before darting across the lawn and pushing past the canvas flaps.

Isla gasped in surprise and stumbled back a step, tripping over the train of her dress. A small couch broke her fall, but Dorian rushed to her side anyway.

"I'm so sorry." He loosed a nervous laugh as he took her gloved hands and pulled her to her feet. "I didn't mean to startle you. I just thought—"

"Captain Gear Heart!" Isla threw her arms around his neck, dragging him in for a hug. Her veil slid over his face, tickling his nose and giving him the urge to sneeze. He made a face to stave it off, enjoying the embrace too much to give it up so easily.

"I've missed you," he said when she finally released him. The comment stole Isla's cheer.

"I've missed you, too." Her eyes watered as they took him in. She swallowed hard before attempting another smile.

"Your father isn't here yet," he said as if she hadn't already noticed.

"I suppose I shouldn't be surprised." Isla sniffled and lifted her chin, though it quivered as she spoke. "My uncle will have to give me away. I doubt he'll mind. He paid for the wedding, after all."

"This is my fault," Dorian admitted, his hand slipping into his pocket. "Ezra really had planned on coming. It's just that…" He held the necklace up, wondering what she would make of it.

"Is that…?" Isla ran a gloved finger down the length of the pendant. "No. It can't be the same one."

"I'm sure it's not," Dorian said, shaking his head sheepishly. "But…when your father saw it…"

"I see." Isla's attention migrated back to his face, her brows pinching. "Poor, Father."

"But he does have a gift for you."

"Oh?"

"At noon," Dorian said. "I shouldn't spoil the surprise any more than that."

Isla smiled and touched the necklace again. "And is this for me, too?" she asked.

Dorian's face felt hot enough to melt butter, and his throat refused to work. He nodded instead, holding up the necklace to her. She turned, inviting him to clasp it around her neck. Then he forgot how to breathe. But his hands moved on their own, fulfilling her wish.

"It's beautiful," she said, looking down at the pendant where it lay over the lace of her wedding gown.

"You're beautiful." The words tumbled from him on the tail of a sigh. It was a desperate sound, and Isla seemed to hear it, too. Her gaze met his, all the humor melting from her expression. "I love you," he blurted before he could stop himself.

"Oh, Dorian…" Isla's gloved hand cupped his cheek, but it was instantly ripped away.

"What the devil do you think you're doing?" Orwell roared, suddenly in the tent with them. "Your groom is waiting out there in front of two hundred people."

"Father's not here yet." Isla's voice quivered as she tried to dislodge her wrist from her uncle's grasp, but he held tight and dragged her toward the part in the canvas.

"He's not coming, you stupid, ungrateful girl," Orwell barked.

"Let go," Isla pleaded. "You're hurting me."

Fury boiled in Dorian's chest, blooming like a stoked furnace as his fists balled at his sides. He was about to do something very stupid, he realized. Something that would probably land him in jail. Or worse.

But before he could act on the impulse, a deafening bell resonated through the tent, and chaos erupted outside.

"What now?" Orwell shoved Isla onto the settee. "Don't move," he ordered before stalking out to investigate.

Dorian had a terrible feeling that he knew exactly what was going on.

"An earthquake?" Isla blinked up at him as if she expected he might have an explanation.

The tent poles rattled as the earth shook them loose. They buckled under the weight of the canvas. Dorian had just enough time to reach her before they were covered in the rough material, trapped while the bell had its way with them.

There was nothing to be done about it except to hold Isla as their world fell apart, yet again.

Chapter Sixteen

December 13th, 1916 – 2:43 p.m.

Dorian was in a mood. Even Kipling had left him be as he'd tightened the fittings on the man's mechanical hand. Dorian's stint in the storeroom had ended with Dr. Doyle's arrival, shortly after Isla took off with Ezra's journal, but his heart had remained behind, bruised and bleeding under the glow of the oraclyst portal.

Isla was not the girl he remembered. Europe had changed her. *Orwell* had changed her.

He downed his ale and grumbled farewell to the others before making the trek back across the city to the empty store where two women had deserted him in one day—and all before lunch. That had to be some sort of record.

The sun dipped behind the buildings as he reached Temple Place, the illumination dusting everything in gloomy shadows. But there was light enough for Dorian to see the broken pane of glass in his front door.

He pulled the flintlock pistol from his waistband and crept inside. The display case was unharmed, the few items of worth still safely tucked within. But a scuffling noise whispered past the jarred door that led to the stairwell.

Dorian followed the sound to the storeroom. He hadn't bothered to lock the door after being rescued, leaving the key jammed in the hole above the handle. What did it matter now that he was out of oraclyst and the journal was gone? Now that Isla was gone.

He slipped past the threshold and discovered a figure in a black coat, riffling through his designs and cluttered piles of tools. An oil lamp sat to one side of the worktable, its dull orange glow melding with the violet light coming from the portal.

Dorian aimed with the pistol, simmering with enough fury to test his loading skills. But then the intruder turned, angling into the lamplight. It spilled across her cheek and illuminated a lock of red hair. Dorian nearly swallowed his tongue. He dropped the pistol to his side and rasped out a noise that crossed somewhere between relieved and livid.

"What the hell are you doing?" he demanded.

Isla yelped and whirled around, pressing her back against the table she'd been searching. Worry tightened the lines of her face. Everyone looked so tired since the Break. Like listless phantoms of their former selves. Or zombies from the tales Kipling shared at the bar about his time in Haiti. Even Boston's Best in their secure infirmary couldn't escape the ravages of the world clock.

"I need the necklace, Dorian," Isla said, regaining some of her composure. "Orwell found your note about it in my father's journal. He says that he can't fix the machine without it."

Dorian snorted. "You've become quite the henchwoman for him, haven't you?"

She blanched at the accusation, but she didn't deny it. The insult was too close to the truth, and neither seemed overly comfortable with the idea.

"He threatened to send the timekeepers to collect the necklace if I don't return with it," Isla said, struggling to look at him. She'd lost the fervor of her first mission into Late Boston. This business was old hat now.

"What else did he threaten?" Dorian sneered. "To throw your *husband* out of the ivory tower to fend for himself amongst us peasants?"

"Please…" Isla closed her eyes. There was no fight in her, but Dorian had enough for both of them.

"Did he promise you more *medicine*? What prize dangles from his hook this time?"

Tears glistened in the corners of her eyes. "I get to keep you alive."

"Don't pretend you're doing this for me." He ground his teeth, resisting the urge to comfort her. She didn't deserve his sympathy. Not after what she'd done to him. "You've already admitted that Orwell is using the captain and your friend as leverage."

"What am I supposed to do, Dorian?" Isla held out her hands. "Let everyone suffer?"

"It's not you causing the suffering—not *their* suffering, anyway," he added, his scowl growing deeper. "You do realize that, don't you?"

"But I could prevent it. So easily. I just have to give him the necklace."

"Is it easy?" Dorian's sharp laugh injured him as much as it seemed to hurt Isla, but once he'd torn the wound open, there was no stanching it. "Whose pain are you really trying to ease?"

Isla scoffed, but the sound was more acceptance than offense. Her hand slipped into the pocket of her coat, and for a brief moment, Dorian wondered if she might pull a pistol of her own. Just how much had her uncle changed her? His heart hammered as he waited to find out.

But then her shaking fingers withdrew a small bottle. The glass was dark but transparent enough for Dorian to see that it was full to the brim.

"Take it," she said, holding it out to him. "I'm sure someone around here would benefit more from it than

I."

Dorian wanted to believe her. He wanted to believe a lot of things.

"I don't have the necklace," he confessed, pushing her hand away.

"No. You must," Isla begged. "Who else could have—?"

"Your father took it with him when he…when he left."

Dorian didn't know how else to explain what had happened that morning. How one strange encounter had changed the course of the day so drastically, splitting it apart like a lightning-struck elm they were all futilely trying to hold together with bits of twine.

Isla's breath rushed out in a quivering sob, but she recovered quickly. She blinked back her tears and glanced around the workshop, her gaze jumping from the lapidary wheel to the ring of oraclyst.

"Then make a new one," she said. "You have all the tools."

"It doesn't matter." Dorian sighed and raked a hand through his hair. "That necklace was unique. Special."

"It was made of oraclyst, and you have plenty here."

"It won't work the same."

"I don't care!" Isla shouted. "It will keep Orwell

from hurting people I love, and that's all that matters. And why shouldn't it work the same?" she added, annoyed curiosity fueling her temper.

"Because that necklace belonged to your mother. She gave it to me herself."

Dorian was sure of it now. There was no other explanation. Elizabeth Huxley had somehow returned from wherever Ezra's machine had sent her. She had been decades older and looser in the head—rattled and haggard as if the future hadn't agreed with her at all.

Isla's hands trembled as she curled them against her chest, clutching the bottle of laudanum. "That's impossible."

"Is it?" Dorian laughed. "Any more impossible than what we've lived through these past three months?"

After the Break, he'd had to train himself to reject reality—or what he'd always assumed reality was. Time no longer cared about reason or rules. Whatever solution existed for the broken timeline, it wouldn't be found within the confines of definitive science.

"You really saw her?" Isla pressed her lips together and took a careful step toward him.

Dorian retreated, backing out of the storeroom. That had been a lesson he only cared to learn once. What she'd done was worse than anything Orwell's timekeepers could do. The world was burning, but he still had his pride. He wouldn't make a new necklace. Not for Isla.

"You need to leave," he said, but the demand fell flat as the three o'clock bell rang out its first note. The building trembled and creaked in response.

Dorian gritted his teeth and braced himself in the doorway of the storeroom. He'd lost track of time. Again. Isla had always had that effect on him, though it had never been so problematic as today. He tried to be angry about it—and for plenty of other things that were well worth being furious over. But when his gaze snagged on her, the fire burned out.

Tears streamed down Isla's face, bringing her agony into sharp focus as the flame of the oil lamp flickered brighter. She leaned against the worktable, hands gripping the edge until her fingers turned white. Her knees buckled with the second toll, and she cried out as she hit the floor.

Dorian felt the weight of the bell, too. The bittersweet pluck at his heartstrings as he remembered the feel of Isla's skin against his. The taste of her swollen mouth. The way she'd breathed his name in the dark, pushing him toward the precipice of everything and nothing.

After three months, he'd thought the memory would

be easier to endure. But it had only gotten worse. Though he savored as much as he suffered. The bells were an acquired misery. One that Isla had remedied with opium. Until now.

The laudanum bottle lay abandoned on the floor.

"Dorian," she whispered, hardly audible over the rattling of machinery and the groaning of the walls. He left his post at the doorway to join her on the floor, dragging her body between his legs and against his chest.

"I've got you," he said, rocking her as the bell tolled its third and final time. "It's almost over."

Enduring the time shifts without his oraclyst goggles was disorienting. Dorian should have been mad at Isla for that, too. But all he could think about was the way the morning light had glowed around her like a halo as he'd helped her climb over the balcony railing at her uncle's house.

In one miraculous timeline, Isla had run away with him, playing Juliet to his Romeo, and they'd spent a few precious hours in each other's arms before time collapsed and began again. Dorian's heart ached with the memory, breaking all over again as he was reminded of what he'd almost had. What he'd maybe *still* have, if he'd been brave enough to come for her more than just that once.

Isla's cool fingers touched his cheek, and he realized he was crying. But then, so was she.

"Please, don't—" he began, pulling her hand away from his face. Isla didn't wait for him to finish, and he forgot what he was saying anyway as her mouth closed over his.

Every nerve in his body was electrified. How long had he wished for this? How many times had the three and nine bells sent him into a masochistic spiral of regret and longing as he'd recounted every moment of that timeline with her? Did she have regrets, as well?

Isla's lips were wet with tears. Dorian cleaned the salt from them with his tongue, enjoying the way her breath quickened as her sobs quelled and turned into something else. This was a new pleasure, not the timid, sweet kisses they'd shared when they'd thought they had all the time in the world.

These were end-of-the-world kisses. And Dorian wanted more.

Isla panted softly as Dorian's mouth migrated across her cheek and then down the column of her neck. One of her hands still grasped his, but her other found its way to his collar. Her fingers hooked over the fabric, grazing his collarbone as she twisted between his legs, offering up more flesh for his roving lips.

When her hot breath grazed his ear, Dorian nearly came out of his skin. His free hand tangled in the laces of her leather vest before venturing farther south, tugging up the folds of her thick skirt. He needed more of her, and he knew this might be his only chance. The next bell could ruin everything. All over again.

"Take me upstairs," Isla purred against his neck.

Chapter Seventeen

September 13th, 1916 – 6:56 a.m.

"I'm so very sorry I'm late," Dorian began, apologizing to Ezra the second he stepped off the elevator. His morning had gone from bad to strange, and considering the look on Ezra's face, Dorian feared it would not be getting better anytime soon.

"Nonsense," Ezra howled cheerfully. "You've arrived just in time. Hurry, hurry!" He waved Dorian deeper into the mechanical room of the Custom House Tower's new clock.

A raised platform held the machine's inner workings, the gear train that dictated the time displayed on the four faces of the tower. Chains ran from the larger wheels, reaching for the back wall where a massive copper barrel punched with square holes rested on a second platform. The landing was attached to the first by a narrow walkway made of old boards.

A loom of cables fed through an opening in the ceiling and stretched above the drum, disappearing into the belfry where Dorian had heard tell of a carillon with dozens of bronze bells that would make the city dance with music. But he suspected these were not the elements of the machine that Ezra had called upon him to inspect.

Six glowing rings of oraclyst boxed in the open space beneath the gear platform. Four sides, a top, and a bottom. Inside the cube, and slightly to the left, swung a long pendulum. A caged stack of cast-iron weights with crystal corner pieces hung to the right.

Copper wires spiraled up the four legs of the platform, crisscrossing like a lattice along the underside and reaching down the length of the pendulum, which Dorian now realized was a dry cell battery. The wires also wrapped around the chain attached to the weights before linking into one of the oraclyst portals.

"I thought you'd given the time travel experiments a rest," Dorian said, his pulse now pounding in his ears.

"Yes, yes," Ezra grumbled. "Well, mostly."

The glowing crystals reminded Dorian of the one the woman on the street had pressed into his hand, and he suddenly remembered where he'd seen the necklace before. He reached into his pocket and fetched the pendant, holding it up to the light that spilled through a narrow window in the corner of the room.

"Where did you get that?" Ezra demanded, the color draining from his face as he took the necklace from Dorian.

"A woman on the street—"

"Elizabeth?" Ezra took a step toward the elevator.

"No." Dorian touched his shoulder, giving it a gentle squeeze. "She was much too old."

"Have you learned nothing, boy?" Ezra shrugged him off with an uncharacteristic snarl. He stalked across the room to stand in front of the glowing cube of ora-clyst and thrust a finger at the machine. "We're tampering with the fabric of time. It's only natural that we encounter travelers from the future at some point. Don't you see what this means?" he said, the malice in his voice shifting into awe and exhilaration.

"What?" Dorian snapped. "What does it mean?"

Ezra slipped through the nearest portal of crystals and held the necklace up as if it were a torch, and he the Statue of Liberty. "It means we must be close. We can't give up now."

Dorian's teeth rattled in his skull as the first knell of the bell struck him like a tuning fork. He slapped his hands over his ears and watched as the glowing crystal portals began to pulse. Crackling arcs of blue voltage leapt from the pendulum bob to the necklace grasped in Ezra's hand. His body writhed as the electricity cut through him before leaping to the hanging weights on the other side of the cube, finishing its circuit.

"Ezra!" Dorian took a step toward the machine, but

then the second peal of the bell clamored through the tower, shaking the entire building. Adrenaline shot through his veins. It quickened his blood until he was consumed by panic.

The air turned violet, the blinding light bleeding out from the portal rings. Dorian turned his face away, hands still pressed over his ears as the crystals intensified with the third toll.

"Dorian!" Ezra's muffled voice cut through the rumbling roar in the tower. "There's still time!"

Dorian squinted at the machine, barely making out his friend's rigid form in the glare of the oraclyst. Electricity still crackled all around him, but he gritted his teeth through the fourth bell.

"Find my journal!" Ezra shouted. "You have to protect it. Swear you will."

Dorian eased an inch closer. "Just come away from the machine," he pleaded.

"Swear it!" Ezra barked.

"I swear it." Dorian ground his teeth as the hairs on his arms stood on end. The air was charged and hot with static. A sickening tendril of dread curled around his spine as he imagined the machine striking him down like lightning smiting a tree.

"It's at the workshop," Ezra said. "You can't let it

fall into the wrong hands."

The warning left little doubt as to what the inventor had planned. But if there had been any question in Dorian's mind, it would have certainly vanished when Ezra began taking inventory of the portals all around him. His gaze settled on the one between them, his mouth and the fingers of his free hand working as he made some silent calculation.

"Don't do it!" Dorian's words were nearly cut off by the fifth toll. "Isla's wedding—" He realized it was a silly thing to worry about when the tower felt as if it might collapse at any second. But come hell or high water, Isla was never far from his thoughts. "You're supposed to walk her down the aisle," he reminded Ezra. "She needs you!"

"No, my boy." Ezra managed a quivering smile, holding it even as the sixth bell ripped through the tower. "She needs *you*."

Dorian sucked in a surprised breath. Was he so transparent? Had Isla's father known his heart all this time? And what on earth could Isla possibly need from a clocksmith that her airship captain fiancé couldn't provide?

These questions and more curdled in his aching mind, but he forgot them all as the seventh bell bellowed overhead.

Before the excruciating resonance had a chance to dispel, Ezra pressed a finger to the side of his nose, stepped through the portal between him and Dorian, and vanished.

Chapter Eighteen

December 13th, 1916 – 5:16 p.m.

Isla found the four and five o'clock bells much easier to endure while tangled in Dorian's bedsheets, with his hands wrapped behind her neck, her waist, and under her thighs.

Every inch of her skin sang with the memory of his touch, a recollection the world clock couldn't wipe away with its infernal tolling. Though the slice of history that belonged to three o'clock was a bit hazy now, as it always was with the passage of time. Like a love letter read in the rain, the ink running and blurring every other word.

But Isla remembered what it said. And now her body did, too.

The laudanum had been forgotten on the storeroom floor, but she happily accepted a cup of coffee and a cold cheese pastry from Dorian—after they finally exhausted themselves. Isla curled herself in the corner opposite him on the large windowsill in the front room, where they enjoyed their meal and watched the snow fall outside.

The sun had set some time ago, and the sky was almost finished shrugging off the last light of dusk. Several windows in the buildings across the street glowed with golden firelight. Orwell had negotiated with the governor to keep the electricity on for the infirmary, but cut off the rest of the city. The new electric streetlamps were useless, forcing the few businesses still in operation to light their storefronts with oil lamps and lanterns.

"Will you hate me when the six o'clock bell comes?" Dorian asked, holding his cup of coffee closer to his chest. His gaze drew up at Isla hesitantly, as if he weren't sure he wanted to know the answer. Or he knew he couldn't trust it.

"No." She smiled sadly. "Though I might hate myself."

"Will you go back to him?"

Isla wasn't sure if he meant her uncle or the captain. Of course, they were both waiting for her at the infirmary.

"You know my uncle will send his men if I don't return." She set her coffee cup on top of a stack of books and wrapped her hands over Dorian's arm, enjoying the warmth of his skin. She wanted to remember the feel of him. There was plenty of time for guilt to gnaw at her heart later. For now, she was determined to enjoy these fleeting moments with Dorian.

"Stay with me," he said, pressing a hand over hers. "There are places in the city we could hide."

"And what of Mabel and the captain? What happens if my uncle solves the riddle of the machine and stabilizes Late Boston in a timeline that includes the vows I took?"

"Did you mean them?" Dorian asked.

"I thought I did," she admitted. "Leopold is a good man. He doesn't deserve to die."

"Orwell wouldn't *really* hurt him to spite you, would he?" A shiver rocked Dorian's shoulders. The stove needed more coal, but it was hard to come by like everything else in Late Boston. Still, Isla doubted the chill in the room was fully to blame for the tremor in his hands.

"My uncle is capable of all manner of unspeakable things."

"Surely the Le Guin family would have something to say about that."

Isla shrugged. "Even so, that leaves the machine. My uncle has a legion of scientists at his disposal. It will take them no time at all to decipher my father's journal. Even without the necklace, they're sure to work out a solution."

"Which timeline do you think Orwell's after?" Dorian asked.

Isla bit her bottom lip. The question was one she'd had plenty of time to ponder in her hospital room, and it made her long for the notes in her own journal. She couldn't be entirely certain, but she had narrowed it down to what she considered the most likely outcomes.

"Le Guin died in all but two timelines," she said, holding up her fingers as she struggled to remember the details her mind refused to retain with the shifting of the bells. "The first and the fifth. If my uncle sees a viable way to fix Late Boston, he'll want to keep the captain alive to lead the Storm Crows to war. Unless…" Her mind reeled at the idea of how much damage a man like Orwell could do with a time machine.

"Unless what?" Dorian pressed.

"Unless the machine is capable of going back farther in time."

"No." He shook his head. "The oraclyst portals only had enough power to rewind the clock six hours. The necklace shorted out a new portal with each time collapse. Ezra made a note about it being out of sync or overcharged…" Dorian paused, and his gaze slid off into nowhere. "As if it had come from some other place," he whispered.

"Or some other *time*, perhaps?" Isla's memories of him giving her the necklace on her wedding day were strongest after eight and two. She'd detailed the gift in her journal but hadn't understood its significance until recently. "You said my mother gave it to you?"

"I was on my way to see your father at the tower before the ceremony," he explained. "Ezra wanted to show me the clock, to have me witness the first ringing of the bell with him." Dorian scratched his head and then stood. He crossed the room to the desk in the corner and fetched a book before returning to the windowsill.

"Another journal?" Isla asked hopefully.

"Mine." Dorian nodded as he flipped through the pages. When he found what he was looking for, he turned the book around and tapped a paragraph. "I had stopped to look in a shop window, and there she was, with wispy gray hair and a dirty skirt. I thought she was a beggar, but then she pressed the spear of oraclyst into my palm and uttered a cryptic message before wandering off into the crowd."

He flipped ahead a few pages and pointed out another paragraph.

"It's the same." Isla's brow creased as he turned to another matching section. "But I should expect so if it was her necklace that caused the Break."

"No, she was only there in five of the six timelines," Dorian said, turning back to the very first entry in the journal. "If the necklace is responsible for the machine's malfunction, where was she in the first timeline? Why did that one collapse, as well?"

"I don't know." Isla shook her head. "None of this makes sense."

"I might know where we can find some answers." Dorian wet his lips, and his eyes lit with a mischievous zeal that reminded Isla of the way her father had looked anytime a new idea struck him. "There's a certain level of risk, of course—"

The sound of muffled voices drew their attention out the window and down to the dark street below. Five men loitered in front of the store. One carried a lantern, and two others had baseball bats slung over their shoulders. They shot wary glances down Temple Place and then looked up at the window. Isla and Dorian moved quickly, retreating from the glass to take shelter in the shadows of the apartment.

"They work for my uncle," Isla whispered. She'd recognized Mr. Bradbury and the man in the paperboy cap who'd collected her from Brewer Fountain. "I've taken too long."

"I might be able to buy us some time." Dorian fetched their coats and his satchel from a wingback chair where they'd discarded them on their way to the bedroom.

"We're all out of time," Isla said, but Dorian only grinned.

"Trust me."

She really wanted to, and she almost did. But then glass shattered in the store below. And not just a small pane like Isla had sacrificed to get inside earlier. It sounded as if every bit of breakable material in the place had just met its untimely end.

They were coming for her. And for Dorian and the necklace he didn't have.

Dorian's fingers laced through Isla's. They stepped lightly as they cut across the apartment and began down the stairs, pressing their backs against the far wall to remain out of sight. The chaos in the store continued with more glass shattering and wood splintering. Isla imagined the display cases and all the lovely clocks and watches, and her heart sank.

Then the door to the storeroom creaked open.

"Jiminy," someone said, following it up with a low whistle. "Bet you ten dollars we find it in here."

Another man grumbled something noncommittal, and then the sounds of destruction doubled as they tore through the secret workshop. Dorian's grip tightened on Isla's hand, and he closed his eyes, wincing as the clatter of tools and the squeal of metal being wrenched apart echoed up the stairwell.

"Dorian, the portal," Isla whispered, wondering how much more quickly her uncle would succeed with a supply of cut and polished oraclyst.

"It's all right," he said. "We don't need it."

"But—"

Dorian pressed a finger to his lips and led her down the stairs. The two men in the workshop were deep enough in the room now that they didn't notice until it was too late. Though Dorian was quieter than Isla had been when he pushed the door closed. He twisted the key in the lock and stuffed it into his pocket, ushering Isla into the corner behind the door that led to the front room as the men trapped in the workshop shouted for help.

All three remaining men came to investigate. Just as soon as they passed the threshold, Dorian and Isla slipped behind them and ran through the store. Their boots crunched on glass, but they didn't stop to take inventory of the damage.

"There they are!" someone shouted.

"Forget the simps. Go get the girl!" Bradbury ordered.

Isla's stomach shot into her throat, and her lungs burned as she struggled to keep up with Dorian. But they didn't dare slow down. The darkness offered cover, and the more they could put between them and her uncle's men, the better.

They retraced their steps back to Washington Street and through Downtown Crossing, minding the cracks and potholes the best they could without light to guide them. For a moment, Isla wondered if they were heading back to the Greasy Gear. But then Dorian turned down Milk Street, dragging her along behind him.

"Orwell keeps more eyes on State Street," he explained, his breath fogging between them. "We'll take the back way to the tower."

The tower?

Isla's mind struggled to follow his logic. Was this where he intended to find answers? How he planned to buy them time? Or had he gone full-blown Shakespeare and planned to see them off in a dramatic and suicidal farewell to the world?

Isla couldn't deny that without opium or Dorian to ease the bells' toll, death would certainly be a tempting option. But that didn't mean she was ready to succumb to it just yet.

"Why are we going to the tower?" she asked breathlessly. Her hand ached in his grip, and she was relieved when they paused near Post Office Square. But the break only lasted for a second.

Boots echoed behind them, and razor-sharp whispers cut through the cold air.

"I think I know where your father is," Dorian whispered as they continued down Milk Street.

Isla knew better than to hope it could be true, but she did anyway. Her breath wheezed as she picked up the pace. They cut up Broad Street and slipped down Central, taking cover in the shadow of the Trade Building across from the Custom House.

She peeked around the corner, spying five more timekeepers standing guard between the pillars at the top of the stairs. Unnatural light spilled down from the tower above, turning the night an eerie purple and illuminating the deep cracks that marred the building's foundation. More fractures spiderwebbed across the cobblestone sidewalks and surrounding streets.

The few electric streetlamps that lined the sidewalk had been converted to oil to offer more visibility for the guards. Not that any sane person would be interested in going inside the building that housed the malfunctioning time machine. Still, her uncle hadn't been willing to take that risk.

Isla wasn't sure *she* was ready to take that risk.

"The elevators won't work with the electricity shut

down," Dorian whispered, stealing a glance back the way they'd come. Isla didn't hear boots any longer, but she was sure it was only a matter of time before Orwell's men found them. Sooner if Dorian thought they would make it past the guards outside the Custom House.

Her gaze drew up the length of the tower, and she swallowed. That many stairs would be hell. At least in her heeled boots. She hitched up her skirt and squatted on the sidewalk to unlace them. It was entirely unlady-like, which made being caught by the likes of Kipling so much worse.

"That you, Doris?" he whispered, holding a small lantern in Dorian's face. "What brings you to these parts? And with the sticky-fingered vamp?" he added, smirking down at Isla.

She huffed and stood upright, clutching her shoes to her chest.

"Aren't you a sight for sore eyes." Dorian grabbed Kipling by the shoulders and kissed the unstitched side of his face. "We need to get inside the tower."

"Have you gone mad?" Kipling shoved him back a step, cringing at the affection. "That machine chews men up and spits 'em out some other place. You said so your-self."

"Yes! We need to get to that other place," Dorian

explained. He dug a watch out of his pocket and flipped open the cover. "And to do that, we have to make it to the machine before the next bell. In exactly twenty-three minutes."

"You're a glutton for punishment." Kipling shook his head. "But so am I. Take me lamp. You're gonna need it in there." He handed the lantern to Dorian and flexed his metal fingers. Then he reached into the pocket of his coat and pulled out three red sticks with long fuses.

Isla's eyes swelled. "Is that…?"

"Sure is, princess." He grinned widely, his sharp eye-teeth glowing in the thin light of the lantern. "Been waitin' for a special occasion to give those clock-knockers a little hell. I suppose now's as good a time as any."

"This is a terrible idea," Isla said as Dorian took her free hand in his again.

"The absolute worst," he agreed. "But we have to try. I can't lose you. Not now. Not like this."

"Aw, come on, Doris." Kipling clicked his tongue. "Don't make me cry afore I have to go rough up these fancy bastards." He opened a panel on the lantern and dipped the ends of the three dynamite fuses inside, sparking them to life. "Wish me luck and mayhem," he said, offering Dorian a two-fingered salute before taking off for the Custom House.

Isla pressed in closer to the side of the Trade Building and watched as Kipling approached the guards. They seemed confused and were slow to reach for the rifles slung over their backs.

"Who goes there?" one shouted, taking aim. Kipling hurled a stick of dynamite, cracking the man in the face. The explosive then rolled across the barrel of the man's rifle before bouncing down the building's front steps.

Another guard fired and missed. The next stick Kipling threw caught the guard in the knee, the flame of the fuse licking at the hem of his coat. His eyes bulged, and he tripped over his feet as he fled his post.

"Take cover!" he yelled to the others. "Get out of here! The whole building could go!"

The guards scattered, tearing off down the dark side streets. One ran down Central, right past Isla and Dorian, as the first explosion sounded from the Custom House. The other two blasts followed soon after.

"I think that's our cue," Dorian said, squeezing Isla's hand. They raced across the street and began up the stairs, mindful of the gaping holes in the concrete.

Isla had expected more damage, especially after the guards' reaction. But the building was in rough enough shape to warrant caution. The quakes that came with the hourly time shifts had claimed more than a few buildings viewable from her room at the infirmary.

"Did you see 'em?" Kipling laughed so hard, he snorted, and his eyes watered. "Off to their mummies!"

A whispery laugh escaped Isla, but her nerves were more to blame than the gutless guards. And possibly the thin layer of wet snow soaking her stockings and freezing her toes.

"I owe you an ale," Dorian shouted as they reached the entrance.

"You owe me more than that!" Kipling wiped the corners of his eyes as his chuckling tapered. Then he waved farewell and took off toward Faneuil Hall.

The guards would return soon. Maybe not the same ones, considering her uncle's distaste for shortcomings. But *someone* would be waiting for them when they came back down from the many, *many* stairs she and Dorian climbed as fast as their feet would carry them.

The lantern flickered in protest at their bounding pace, but Isla could almost hear the ticking of the clock now. The next bell would be upon them in a matter of minutes, and she still had no idea what Dorian had planned.

He'd told her to trust him. Did she? She kept asking herself that. Was following him across the city in the dark of night trust? Was letting him drag her to the top of a tower with no escape trust? Was that what this unhinged, chaotic feeling swelling within her was called?

"Dorian?" she panted, her legs burning from the merciless climb.

"We're nearly there," he promised. "Just a few more floors."

"And then what?" she begged. "How is the machine going to take us wherever it took my father if we don't have the necklace?"

"Your mother returned before he left," Dorian said as they curled around another landing and started up the next flight of stairs. "She was here before the machine malfunctioned. Which means she must have returned through the portal at the workshop."

"What difference does that make?"

"The electricity at the workshop was shut off the month before."

"That shouldn't have mattered," Isla said. "Father used dry cells."

"At first," Dorian agreed. "But for later trials, he connected the portal to the grid, thinking more power was the answer."

"And?"

Dorian winced. "It didn't end well—hence the city revoking his electricity privileges."

"Then how could my mother have come through the portal?" Isla pressed.

"Do you remember what I said about your father's note on the crystal being out of sync or overcharged? What if… What if it had enough charge to power the portal all on its own?"

"Do you think that technology is possible wherever or *whenever* my mother came back from?"

"It must be. It had to be."

"But how does that help us *now?*"

Dorian released her hand as they entered the mechanical room. He set the lantern down on a crate just inside the entrance and opened his satchel, retrieving a chunk of broken crystal.

"If your mother's necklace is the key, maybe a piece of the portal it charged will be enough."

"That's a big *if*," Isla said, more to herself than to Dorian as she followed him deeper into the room.

The violet-tinted darkness was brighter here, lit by her father's latest and most dangerous creation. It shamed her to admit that she still found his work beautiful, the way he blurred the lines between science and art, nature and machine.

"What's that?" she asked, nodding at a copper drum behind the platform over the oraclyst portals.

"Your wedding gift." Dorian said, a pained smile pinching the corners of his mouth. "It was supposed to play your favorite song at noon, after the main bell announced the time, but the first timeline collapsed before it had the chance."

"My favorite song?"

"The one from Swan Lake."

Isla dropped her shoes and covered her face with both hands, trying to smother her sobs. She was tired of hating her father, and tired of hating the person she'd become. But maybe there was still time to make things right. She had to hope.

Dorian's fingers wove through her hair. He sighed and pressed a kiss to her forehead, then another to her lips as her hands fell away from her face.

"Come on," he whispered, leading her toward the machine.

They stepped through a glowing portal and wedged themselves between a swinging pendulum and a stack of hanging weights. It was a tight fit, forcing their bodies flush. Isla wrapped her arms around Dorian's waist as he held up the piece of broken oraclyst.

Time seemed to slow as the final seconds ticked away.

"I might not know what I'm doing," Dorian

confessed, the first real hints of doubt creasing his face. "There's a chance this won't work, or that it could make everything worse."

Isla tightened her arms around his waist. She'd made it this far with him on nothing more than hope and trust. "I'd rather not know what I'm doing with you than have the designs to a life with anyone else," she said.

His breath trembled and danced across her cheek as he leaned down to kiss her one last time. Isla wasn't sure if it was for good luck or a goodbye. It didn't matter either way. She'd made up her mind.

The clock struck six, and the first bell reverberated through the tower.

Isla's teeth chattered, and her bones felt as if they might shake free of her skin and dance away. The oraclyst pulsed all around them, and arcs of blue electricity filled the tight space between the pendulum and the weights, sizzling and popping as it nipped at their skin.

The chunk of oraclyst clutched in Dorian's hand vibrated, but he held tightly to it as he nudged Isla toward a glowing portal. Would she find her father on the other side? There was only one way to find out.

They stepped through the ring of glowing crystals, vanishing before the second bell rang out.

Chapter Nineteen

September 13ᵗʰ, 1916 – 7:24 a.m.

Isla wasn't ready to be married.

Not to Captain Le Guin, no matter how charming everyone found him. Even Mabel was smitten. Isla could tell in the way she giggled excitedly about a honeymoon that wasn't hers, teasing her about bedroom fantasies that were too private for polite company.

"Is that sausage I smell?" Mabel asked, her nose lifting higher. "Seems a bit early."

Isla nodded. "Breakfast is served with morning tea. Uncle likes to begin the workday early and doesn't care to be interrupted again until lunch."

"Barbaric," Mabel grumbled. "But no, you mustn't stoop to dressing yourself."

She slid off the bed and went to the French doors that led out to the balcony, pulling back the curtains to reveal the green and gold treetops of the garden across the street. Two rows of lavenders—purple glass panes Boston's Best had acquired in the last century—bookended the view, leftover from her uncle's latest remodeling project.

A startled yelp leapt from Mabel's throat as she

scrambled away from the French doors and back to the bed. It sent Isla bolting upright, her heart fluttering like a caged bird until she saw Dorian's face.

She climbed over her friend and unlatched the French doors, hushing Mabel's timid protests before throwing her arms around Dorian's neck.

"Captain Gear Heart." She laughed in his ear. "What are you doing here?"

"Plundering treasure," Dorian rasped in a pirate accent. "What else?"

The past five years had filled out his lanky limbs and sharpened the line of his jaw. But his cheeks still flushed when he smiled at her, and his gaze softened as he looked her over. Was he taking comfort in the familiar and appreciating the new in her, as well? A twinge of guilt punished her conscience for how much she hoped.

"It's been far too long," he said, scooping her into a hug so tight that she could feel his heartbeat thumping against her chest. Which made her realize that she was still in her dressing gown.

"I can't believe you're here," she admitted, reluctantly pulling away from him. Tears dripped from her lashes, and she wondered when she had begun to cry—*why* she had begun to cry.

"What's the matter?" He cupped her cheek and

thumbed away a tear as it trailed down her face.

"Nothing! Nothing. It's just so good to see you," she said.

"Is it?" An eager, brave light sparked behind his eyes. Another new development, Isla decided, shivering at the thrill the look sent through her.

"Of course it is." She laughed.

"Then see more of me," Dorian begged. He took her hands and curled them against his chest. "Please, Isla. I may not be a real captain or be able to offer a life of luxury—but I love you. I always have."

"Do you mean it?" Her insides melted at the possibility. Could she really leave this life behind and claim the one she'd dreamt of ever since she was old enough to understand heartache and longing?

"I mean it more than I've ever meant anything in my life," Dorian answered. He released one hand to cup the back of her head, pulling her in until their lips met in an aching kiss. It stole what was left of her breath and set her to panting as soon as he pulled away.

Her childhood crush had seemed a thing long lost, abandoned somewhere along the voyage across the Atlantic, drained from her like the tears she'd shed for her mother. Seeing Dorian again tore away the bandage over her heart, letting the hopes of her youth leak through and make a mess of the future her uncle had so meticulously curated for her.

Mabel cleared her throat from the bed. Isla had completely forgotten about her friend, but the giddy grin on her face suggested she had fresh fantasy fodder to add to Madam Pittard's novel romances.

"I'll let the captain down gently," Mabel promised as she crossed the room to the closet. She returned with a dress that Isla eagerly accepted her help pulling on over her dressing gown. Isla slipped on a coat without finishing her dress buttons and stuffed her feet into a pair of boots.

Mabel blew her a kiss as she and Dorian slipped through the French doors. They climbed over the railing, maneuvered down a garden trellis, and escaped to freedom.

Isla didn't care what came next. Not as long as she had Dorian.

And she did. At least for a little while.

Chapter Twenty

December 13ᵗʰ, 1916 – 7:12 p.m.

Pearl was tired of not being taken seriously. She held the notebook up to the head surgeon and tapped her finger on the list of supplies she needed. Dr. McCaffrey had detailed how little morphine they had left, but Pearl was certain she could help them make it last for at least another month if they would only *listen*.

There were several patients at the infirmary that she was quite eager to begin working on. Many who had been in comas since the Break. She could give them their lives back—or at least, some fraction of their former lives. If only the staff would help collect the necessary tools and equipment.

What little she'd brought with her from the Clockwork Apothecary was nowhere near enough, but it was nothing so expensive or difficult to come by that Boston's Best shouldn't have been able to manage it.

Pearl finally gave up trying to reason with the head surgeon and went in search of McCaffrey. The woman had been evading her all day, but Pearl didn't think it was entirely deliberate. Something had happened. The infirmary was abuzz with whispers. Pearl's skin crawled with them.

A kind nurse stopped to read the question about McCaffrey's whereabouts scrawled in Pearl's notebook and gave her directions to Mr. Orwell's office. She hadn't met the man yet, but Dorian had never had nice things to say about him. Not after he'd paid for Isla to go to school in Switzerland.

Pearl had expected to bump into the Huxley girl by now. The infirmary wasn't a terribly large building, and she'd explored every floor and room, taking stock of the patients that would require the most extensive work. Captain Le Guin was of particular interest to her.

As she neared the hallway that led out of the treatment wing and into the original portion of the State House, a vicious tantrum caught her ear and slowed her steps.

"Check every building if you have to!" a man shouted. "Go door to door. They can't have just *vanished*. I want her back here now! Put three men on that clock store. Just in case they return."

"Yes, sir," another man answered.

"You're wasting time and resources, Mr. Orwell," McCaffrey said. "Let Isla have her fun with the clock-smith. We should be focusing on the journal and the machine."

Dorian. Pearl's heart skipped. They were after Dorian and Ezra's daughter.

"You slipped her a bottle of laudanum," Orwell accused. "Did you think I wouldn't find out? The nurses keep a closer eye on inventory now that supplies are running low."

McCaffrey sniffed. "We have Miss Shelley on staff now. Her clockwork therapies should help make the opiates stretch a while longer."

"Just keep her away from the captain," Orwell grumbled. "He's right where I want him for the moment—out of my way. If the laboratory unlocks the secrets of the time machine, I may have no use for him at all."

Pearl backed quietly down the hall, retracing her steps before she was caught. She didn't need to hear any more. Coming here had been a terrible mistake. Dorian was in danger. They all were if someone like Abraham Orwell took control of the time machine.

She considered leaving the infirmary, but with the number of guards watching the place, she didn't think that was something she'd be allowed to do without Orwell's express permission. And it didn't sound like he parted with assets willingly. He sounded content enough to dispose of people when they no longer served his purpose—like the poor captain.

Thinking of Le Guin put an awful idea in Pearl's head, but she was on her way to his room before she could think of a reason not to wake an ally in this place. She would need help getting out of there. And he needed someone more invested in his survival.

Chapter Twenty-One

September 13ᵗʰ, 1916 — 6:00 a.m.

It hurt every time. Not only in Ezra's body but also in his brain. In his pride, and deep within his heart.

He didn't belong in this timeline. He didn't belong in any of them. He was just a stupid, dangerous man who had ruined everything. The portal at the stub-end terminal of Court Street Station was a painful reminder. As if his conscience would ever allow him to forget.

Ezra picked himself up off the tunnel floor and reached into the darkness until his hand found concrete. He followed the familiar, rough cracks in the wall to a fissure where he'd tucked away a carbide headlamp, a pail, and a pickaxe. His last set of supplies. He would have to replace them before the machine's next cycle. He couldn't afford to waste time.

He struck the flint on the headlamp and turned the dial until it lit up the abandoned station, including a collapsed section of tunnel that revealed a trove of raw oraclyst. The violet quartz grew like moss, blanketing every surface of the hidden cave with its shimmering splendor. It made Ezra's skin prickle with both dread and awe.

Whenever his mind went soft with exhaustion, he imagined a great dragon curled up in the middle of the trove, guarding its treasure from knights in shining armor. Sometimes, he saw Isla and Dorian as children, playing among the crystals in paper pirate hats, swinging pretend swords at pretend sea monsters.

But most of all, he saw Elizabeth. The horror and surprise on her face, right before the crystals had stolen her from this world. Twice.

Whispers echoed through the oraclyst, fragments of memories that Ezra wasn't sure were his or someone else's. They lured him inside, welcoming him to their secrets if he dared to untangle them. There was plenty for what he needed, though it was tedious work harvesting and hauling the crystals back through the tunnels.

Ezra would have liked Dorian's help. He'd even ventured up to the surface once to see the boy in this timeline, but just for a moment. There were only three hours between time shifts in this place, and he couldn't afford to waste them. Besides, he was too ashamed to tell Dorian where he was or what he was doing. And he was too afraid that Orwell would find out and put a stop to it.

He couldn't let that happen. Elizabeth's life depended on his work—even if it had been her undoing in the first place. He'd let her down once before. Twice, if he counted this latest miscalculation. And he did.

But he knew what he was doing now. He knew where he'd gone wrong. If he could only keep at it a little longer, he could make things right again. At least, in one timeline.

Ezra collected his pail and pickaxe and set to work, chipping away at the oraclyst that had chipped away at his life. It was a score he feared he might never settle.

But only time would tell.

In the darkness he'd left behind, the oraclyst portal pulsed vibrantly. An electric spark danced a circle around the crystals. Six times. And then two newcomers stepped through the ring and into the tunnel.

Epilogue

September 13th, 1911 – 11:57 a.m.

A frown tugged at Isla's lips as she watched her uncle hobble up the loft stairs behind her mother. She hadn't expected to see him for another few weeks, closer to her birthday, when he would undoubtedly lecture her parents on the feminine etiquette he claimed she was sorely lacking.

Such nonsense.

Etiquette was *not* an essential field of study. Isla much preferred her father's science lessons on the tinkering floor. And she was certainly lady enough with her mother and Winnie's mentoring in between literature and history lessons. Both had spent time in fancy boarding schools for girls. They'd learned how to host high teas and dinner parties, how to curtsey should they ever encounter royalty on holiday abroad.

But what did Isla care about parties and princes? She knew how to hold her hands in polite company, knew to speak softly and smile at the stuffed-shirt investors who dropped by the workshop to inspect her father's designs. Even as they looked down their noses—or turned them up with distaste.

"You're related to Abraham Orwell?" Dorian whispered, peeling his gaze away from the stairs as soon as they were alone.

Isla nodded. "My uncle. Though we hardly see him." She removed her hat and fingered back a loose curl before catching Dorian's stare at her neckline.

"What is it?" She touched the lace along her collar. "Did I spill coffee on my frock?"

"No… I mean… I don't think so." His ears turned bright red as his gaze shot up to meet hers.

"Are you well, Dorian? You seem out of sorts."

Before he could answer, her uncle's booming voice filtered down from the loft.

"She belongs at a finishing school! How do you expect her to find a proper husband after the way you've brought her up here—just shy of a feral cat."

Dorian's throat bobbed as he swallowed, and Isla wondered what his skin would feel like against her lips. "A finishing school? Like the ones for court ladies over in Europe?" he asked.

"Don't worry." Isla laughed, unable to hide the satisfied grin aching in her cheeks. His concern stirred something low in her belly. "They've had this argument before. Mother and Father are entirely opposed. I'm not going anywhere. Besides, Winnie's lessons are far more useful than any of the silly things they teach at those charm schools."

As far as future husbands were concerned, Isla had no intention of marrying a bachelor of Boston's Best, as she'd overheard her uncle suggest to her mother the last time he'd dropped by. The boys from those families were trained like show poodles and schooled within an inch of their personalities. If they weren't congratulating themselves on their effortless pedigree, they were busy butchering Latin as they misquoted philosophers who would have found them as boorish and pretentious as Isla did.

Dorian, on the other hand, didn't know a lick of Latin. Isla knew it was an absurd quality to swoon over, but there wasn't much about the clocksmith's son that didn't amuse or excite her. He'd even managed to charm her parents.

The arguing in the loft shifted to her father's latest invention, drawing Dorian's attention away with it. "It sure is…*unusual*. Do you know what it does?"

"I do." Isla's grin deepened. She clutched her hat closer and whispered, "It's a time machine."

Dorian was even more handsome when he pouted. "We're a little old for make-believe," he grumbled.

"I'm serious." She laughed again, bubbling with

good cheer that even a visit from her uncle couldn't upset.

Her father had really done it this time. Well, had *almost* done it. It wouldn't be long now. Ezra Huxley was a name that would go down in history. Isla just knew he was onto something big. Something that would change the world forever.

She didn't understand all the finer details, but she'd followed along well enough to give Dorian a rough idea of how the machine worked. He listened skeptically, occasionally rolling his eyes until she held up a bit of the crystal her father had used to make the portal ring, letting it catch in the sunlight that spilled through the glass atrium ceiling.

"What do you see?" she asked Dorian, watching as his eyes grew wide with astonishment. "Something that's happened already? Or something that's yet to transpire?"

Dorian's hand wrapped her wrist and tugged the crystal closer to his face. The motion curled her body around his shoulder, where she rested her cheek and searched the quartz for whatever had sparked his interest.

The bits of purple stone her father left lying around the tinkering floor had only ever given her glimpses of incidents a few moments into the past or future. Her father's machine was intended to amplify that effect—and transport one *to* those distant times. She wasn't quite sure how it all worked, but Dorian seemed about as interested in her elementary ramblings on crystallography and physics as she was in poodles and philosophers.

Something crashed upstairs, startling Isla from the cozy spot she'd found against Dorian's backside. Then her mother appeared on the landing above, face red and creased with annoyance. Isla's uncle was the only one who seemed to have that effect on her. Not even the snobbiest, most insulting benefactors could summon a cross word from Elizabeth Huxley.

"I'm telling you, it's possible," she shouted, grasping her hips with both hands. "We can prove it."

"I didn't come here for a performance," Orwell barked as he emerged from the loft entrance. He stabbed his cane down at the machine below. "You can save the theatrics for the crystal-ball-gazing carnival-goers. That's the only paying audience you'll find in this city."

"It's nearly ready for a test run," Ezra called over Orwell's shoulder. "We'll need a volunteer subject, naturally. I'm sure I'll be able to round up a reliable chap within a day or two."

"We don't need a volunteer for *this* demonstration." Isla's mother made for the stairs, but Orwell snatched her by the sleeve.

"For once, I agree with your husband. Don't be a fool, Elizabeth!"

"You already think me one, so what does it matter?" She bared her teeth at him and wrenched her arm free. The landing trembled, and she staggered back a step.

Isla's breath caught in her throat as if she might scream a warning, but she couldn't get her mouth to work. She couldn't get anything to work as she watched her mother tumble over the loft railing and plummet toward the tinkering floor far below.

Blue electricity crackled up from the machine, bouncing off the crystals. For a moment, Isla imagined the arcs threading across the gap to create a safety net like the ones used by flying trapeze artists at the circus.

It was an impossible, childish wish that quickly dissolved as the machine made a horrific popping sound, and her mother slipped past the ring, collapsing onto the tinkering floor like a discarded ragdoll.

"Elizabeth!" Isla's father shoved past Orwell and rushed down the loft stairs.

"Mother?" Isla reached her first. Her hands trembled as she tried to decide where was safe to put them. A trickle of blood ran from her mother's ear, and the ruffled hem of her dress had hitched up to her thighs, revealing her heeled boots and stocking garters. Tears blurred Isla's vision. She couldn't seem to pull enough air into her lungs.

"Elizabeth?" Ezra knelt on her opposite side across from Isla. His voice quivered helplessly, but his hands went to work right away, feeling her neck for a pulse. She whimpered softly at his touch.

"Mother?" Isla reached for her hand.

"Thank heavens." Orwell sighed from the foot of the loft stairs. He leaned heavily on his cane and ran a silk handkerchief over his face, wiping away sweat or tears. Isla wasn't sure which, but he looked relieved, nonetheless.

"My shoulder," Elizabeth groaned. "And my head," she added as her eyes cracked open. She tried to sit upright, and a hiss whistled past her teeth. "Oh, and definitely my leg."

Ezra placed a hand on the back of her neck and helped lower her to the floor again. "Just…take it easy, darling."

The bells over the door rattled as Dorian bound back inside the workshop.

"An ambulance is on the way," he announced, panting as he regained his breath.

Isla hadn't realized he'd left. Her mind was still stiff

with alarm, even as it flooded with relief.

Her mother was alive. She wasn't in great shape, but she was alive. She would live.

The bells at the door jingled again, and several medics rushed inside. Isla stood and backed out of their way, giving them room to inspect her mother's injuries before carefully moving her onto a stretcher. Her uncle and father watched with tender gazes, and Isla was struck by how remorseful they both looked.

"She won't be able to manage the stairs as she recovers," Ezra said. He raked his fingers through his hair and tore off his goggles before dragging his hand down his face.

"A workshop is no place for a family, anyway," Orwell grumbled. But then his tone softened. "That could have been much worse."

"I'm aware." Ezra swallowed, and Isla realized he was holding back tears.

"Please," Orwell said, surprising her as much as her father. It was not a word she thought her uncle knew. "Let us end this feud. Come back to work for me. I'll triple your salary. You'll be able to afford a proper house—one that's *safe* and comfortable for your family—*our* family."

Ezra hung his head. "I'll have to speak to Elizabeth

about it."

"Elizabeth would follow you to the gates of hell, and you know it." Orwell scoffed. "You also know that I'm doing this for her sake. And Isla's. You can have your own division if that's what it will take."

"Fine, but I won't leave her side as long as she's in the hospital," Ezra insisted.

"I would expect nothing less," Orwell agreed. "Isla can stay with me until Elizabeth is released—and I'll have my real estate man see what properties are available near the lab…"

Their voices trailed off as they followed the medics outside, where they loaded Elizabeth into the ambulance. Isla lingered behind, her attention having shifted to Dorian. His brows puckered as his gaze fell to meet hers.

"You're going to live with your uncle," he said, almost as if it were a question. "Do you… Do you think we'll…?"

Isla threw her arms around his waist as she had when they were children, forgetting the few years in between when they'd begun to grow into the adults they would soon be. Manners were for strangers and casual encounters, not good friends and life-or-death ordeals. She pressed her cheek against his neck and choked out a miserable sob as his arms wrapped around her back.

His chin grazed her temple, and he pulled her closer. "Don't worry. They'll take good care of your mother at the hospital."

Isla thought so too, but her nerves were still raw, and now an ugly knot of guilt was making short work of her insides. Because as concerned as she was for her mother, her tears were entirely selfish.

"Isla!" her uncle called from the street outside. "Where on earth is that girl?"

She sniffled sharply and pulled away from Dorian as if they were doing something wrong and about to be caught. If her uncle spotted them in such an embrace, he would no doubt claim as much.

Isla took a step toward the open door. Her chest heaved, anxiety gripping her heart like a fist. Everything was happening too quickly. Her mother was going to the hospital, and she was going to live with her uncle. No more lessons on the tinkering floor. No more deliveries from Dorian.

A bleak future ripped through her mind as blinding hot and out of control as the electric arcs crackling about her father's machine—a device that would no doubt find its way to the top of the rubbish heap once her father went back to work for her uncle.

She turned around suddenly and slipped her hands inside the armholes of Dorian's waistcoat, pulling him to her mouth for a tear-soaked kiss. His pulse kicked against her fingers, tucked snuggly between the layers of wool and linen he wore. She thought they felt right there. At home.

"Isla!" her father called out next.

She released Dorian and fled through the open door, wondering when she would see the clocksmith's son again. *If* she would see him again.

Their story couldn't be over. The idea felt wrong and left a sour taste in her mouth. Or maybe that was only her tears, cutting through the sweetness of the stolen kiss.

No, she decided. Their story was not over.

They would find each other again.

It was only a matter of time.

GEAR HEARTS

WORLD CLOCK JOURNALS BOOK TWO

Time can't heal these wounds.

At least, not with a broken time machine ripping them open again and again, every hour on the hour.

Pearl Shelley thought that leaving the Clockwork Apothecary to help Dr. McCaffrey at the Post Boston Infirmary would take her mind off Dorian and the future she can never have with him. But when she discovers a sinister plot to salvage the malfunctioning time machine and use it to hold the world hostage, Pearl knows she must brave the heartache of Late Boston once again. Though she will need help...

The last thing Captain Leopold Le Guin remembers is watching his blushing bride-to-be walk down the aisle— right before the earth split open beneath them and the world went black. After waking to discover that he's been in a coma for the past three months and everyone in the city is in mortal peril—including his new wife— he accepts Miss Shelley's plea for assistance to locate the one man who might be able to help shut down the machine before it's too late: his new father-in-law, Ezra Huxley.

ACKNOWLEDGMENTS

I'm well aware that writing about *anything* requires a heap of research. That said, tackling Cursed Cogs has given me new respect for historical fiction. Technology, science, architecture, etiquette, fashion, and so much more has undergone enormous transformation over the past century. And cities, especially old ones, grow and evolve. Roads are renamed, buildings demolished, and monuments moved.

When covid canceled my research trip to Boston, I had to rely on the internet and the kindness of Bostonians willing to answer my random questions about their city and structures. Special thanks to Northeast Historic Film whose collection includes a 1903 trolley ride through Boston, and to historian Anthony Sammarco who created a series of fantastic videos for the Boston Herald (and a heap of awesome books) about the history of Boston. I am also grateful to the staff at the Marriott Vacation Club Pulse in the Boston Custom House for humoring my more obscure questions about their floorplan and tower features. I hope to visit soon to admire the clock that inspired the Huxley time machine in person.

As always, I am eternally grateful to the veterans of my inner circle: my husband, Paul, who serves as sounding board, beta reader, and the glue that holds life together when I'm neck-deep in a story; my son, Xavier, who intuitively knows when I need encouraging hugs and kisses; my cover designer, Rebecca Frank, who blows me away with her gorgeous work; my sweet, patient editor, Chelle Olson, who keeps my prose neat and tidy; THE professor, George Shelley, who continues to proofread my work and offer much appreciated feedback despite my wandering away from Lana and Limbo City (though I'll be returning soon!); my critique group, the Four Horsemen of the Bookocalypse, whose works and friendship inspire my own; and my Facebook gang of Grim Readers, who kept me sane through quarantine after so many live events were canceled last year. Here's hoping the future has better things in store for us all.

About the Author

USA Today bestselling fantasy author **Angela Roquet** is a great big weirdo. She lives in Missouri with her husband and son in a house stuffed with books, toys, skulls, owls, and glitter-speckled craft supplies. Angela is a member of SFWA and HWA, as well as the Four Horsemen of the Bookocalypse, her epic book critique group, where she's known as Death. When not swearing at the keyboard, she enjoys boating with her family at Lake of the Ozarks and reading books that raise eyebrows.

You can find Angela online at
www.angelaroquet.com

If you enjoyed this book, please leave a review. Your support and feedback are greatly appreciated!